THE SMUGGLERS OF DEAL

Michael Aye

CW00547311

THE SMUGGLERS OF DEAL

MICHAEL AYE

BITINGDUCK PRESS
ALTADENA, CA

Published by Boson Books
An imprint of Bitingduck Press
ISBN 978-1-938463-92-1
eISBN 978-1-938463-93-8
© 2020 Michael Fowler
All rights reserved
For information contact
Bitingduck Press, LLC
Altadena, California
notifications@bitingduckpress.com
http://www.bitingduckpress.com
Cover art by Mike Benton

BOOKS BY MICHAEL AYE

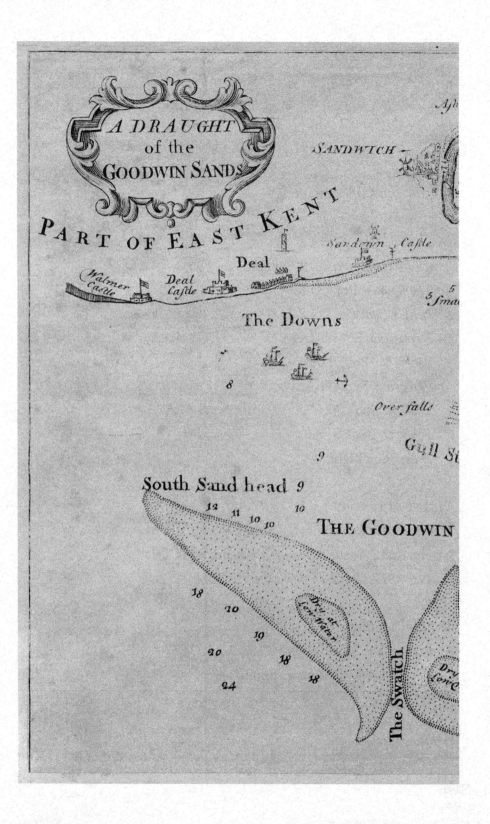

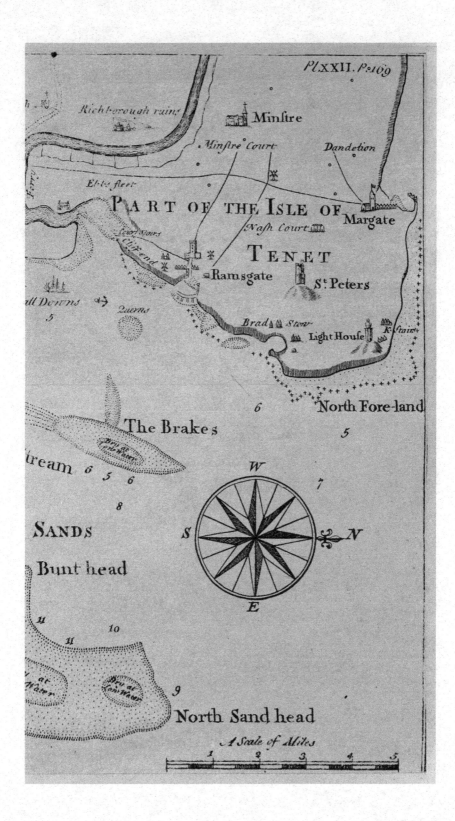

THE DOWNS

Fingleshan
Knowlton
DEAL
Sholden
Betteshanger
Northbourne
Great
Mongeham
Up.
Deal
anstone
Eythorne
Ripple
Walmer
Sutton
Kingsdown
Waldershare Park
Ringwold
West Langdon
ROMAN ROAD
Martin Mill
Sta
Whitfield
East Langdon
West Cliffe
Guston
DOVER DEAL RY
St. Margarets
Lighthouses
Buckland
Charlton
DOVER
229
159
144
60
90
282
350
213

A Smuggler's Song

If you wake at midnight, and hear a horse's feet,
Don't go drawing back the blind, or looking in the street,
Them that ask no questions isn't told a lie.
Watch the wall my darling while the Gentlemen go by.

Five and twenty ponies
Trotting through the dark
Brandy for the Parson, 'Baccy for the Clerk.
Laces for a lady; letters for a spy,
Watch the wall my darling while the Gentlemen go by.

Running round the woodlump if you chance to find
Little barrels, roped and tarred, all full of brandy-wine,
Don't you shout to come and look, nor use 'em for your play.
Put the brishwood back again – and they'll be gone next day!

If you see the stable-door setting open wide;
If you see a tired horse lying down inside;
If you mother mends a coat cut about and tore;
If the lining's wet and warm – don't you ask no more!

If you meet King George's men, dressed in blue and red,
You be careful what you say, and mindful what is said.
If they call you "pretty maid," and chuck you 'neath the chin,
Don't you tell where no one is, nor yet where no one's been!

Knocks and footsteps round the house – whistles after dark –
You've no call for running out till the house-dogs bark.
Trusty's here, and Pincher's here, and see how dumb they lie
They don't fret to follow when the Gentlemen go by!

If you do as you've been told, 'likely there's a chance,
You'll be give a dainty doll, all the way from France,
With a cap of Valenciennes, and a velvet hood –
A present from the Gentlemen, along 'o being good!

Five and twenty ponies,
Trotting through the dark
Brandy for the Parson, 'Baccy for the Clerk.
Them that asks no questions isn't told a lie
Watch the wall my darling while the Gentlemen go by!

by Rudyard Kipling

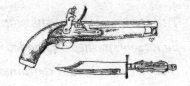

PROLOGUE

L EIF AND MATTHEW ERIKSSON WERE *leaving the Cock and Bull. Frawley, one of Constable Oaks' men, sidled up to the two of them from the shadows.*

"Don't turn around," he hissed. "The duty men have word of the landing tonight. Mr. Stephenson said to warn you."

Leif did not particularly like Stephenson, though he found women for the man. He was repaid by coin, and at times warnings such as what just transpired. The man seemed to have a system in place where intelligence filtered in on a routine basis. Just how many men he bribed with coin, and sometimes women, was anybody's guess.

Frawley whispered, as he left, "Have a care. You are being watched." Then he faded into the shadows at the side wall of the tavern.

Leif whispered to his brother, "I've got to warn Paddy O'Hare somehow."

"Stay here," Matthew said. "I'll sound the alarm and then go home."

Leif then loudly announced, "Damme, Matt. I forgot to get some cigars."

Matthew threw up his hand, mounted his horse and rode off.

***

THE SPOTSMAN MADE HIS SIGNAL and the lugger closed with the shore. Boats soon pushed off, loaded with casks of brandy, hogsheads of tobacco, bales of silk, and containers of tea. Tubmen with straps over their shoulders and backs waited anxiously. It was always this way. Some of them whispered to their friends to kill the time until the boats landed. Then with cargo on their backs and shoulders, they'd haul it from the beach to the waiting pack horses and wagons. One of the tubmen laughed at something witty.

"Shut yer trap or I'll close it for you," a batman said. "I'd never hear a duty man approaching with all yer bloody banter." The tubman drew quiet.

The batman had a pistol and musket as well as a blade. He wanted no truck with the sod. Maybe, he's a bit anxious himself, the tubman thought.

The sound of the surf made the tubman look. A boat came in and was pushed further ashore by a wave. The men were quickly loaded and started their climb up the hillside. The path was steep, had switchbacks and one had to be careful of crumbling rocks that would put a man arse over kettle in a blink.

***

ONCE HE WAS OUTSIDE OF town, Matthew put his horse into a gallop. Time was short and if he didn't sound the alarm quickly enough, good men would wind up in prison, or worse. As he rode, Matthew thought about the constable's man, Frawley. How good was his warning? Should he be believed? What if he got caught? So what...he was not a smuggler. The magistrate may put him on trial but what could they prove? He was restless and went for a ride after he left the tavern. Matthew slowed his horse. He was close now. He didn't want to risk getting shot by a batman, by charging up unexpectedly.

***

DUTY MEN UNDER THE COMMAND of Captain Letchworth had been in place the better part of an hour. An anonymous tip had come in that day. This one was written and was in a woman's handwriting, with no signature on the note. There never was with notes like this. Did she have a grudge against the smugglers? There was more than one widow whose husband had been a riding officer and had been killed in the line of duty. Those women would certainly have a reason to see the smugglers pay. Letchworth also thought, or was it some jilted lover who had been done wrong by a smuggler. Regardless, Letchworth had notified the magistrate, who had agreed that they should act on it.

Letchworth watched from his vantage point as men made their way up the cliff, unloaded their burdens and headed back down to the beach. Two more boats had just landed. He would let the men unload the cargo and head back up the path to the waiting wagons and pack animals. He would then spring his trap, since tired men put up less of a fight.

***

MATTHEW HAD NOW SLOWED HIS horse to a walk. He thought about singing out to gain attention to himself, but that might also alert the duty men should they be drawing near. He took one more puff on his cigar. It was a good cigar; he thought as he looked at the ash. Damme, his horse suddenly shied, almost toppling him from the saddle. Ash fell from the cigar as Matthew took one last deep puff from the cigar. He never thought the ember of the lit cigar might serve as a warning to anyone that a rider was approaching.

Four men were hidden behind a couple of boulders. They were waiting on Leif Eriksson. He was the man who set up the smuggling operations. If they got him, it would hurt the operation, at least for a while. Seeing the glow from the cigar, the men grew ready.

"Now," the sergeant yelled.

Four musket balls found their mark and thudded into Matthew Eriksson's chest, knocking him off his horse. He was dead before he hit the ground. Death had never occurred to him before the gunshots rang out. His last thought had been to sound the alarm and hurry home to his wife's bed.

The sound of gunfire on the road was the signal. Gunfire then erupted along the path and on the beach. Shouts and curses echoed in the dark. Orange flames spat out, signaling the locations of shooters. Others fired back at the flashes. On the beach the boats, only partially unloaded, shoved off. One man was pushing a boat further into the water. He cried out and threw up his hand as blood gushed from his mouth. Falling into the surf, he thought, 'Oh, Sadie.' The fighting soon ended. They'd captured fifteen men. At least three of the smugglers were dead. Three plus Leif Eriksson.

Sergeant Duncannon carried a torch as he and Captain Letchworth went to see the body of Leif Eriksson. Only it wasn't Leif. It was his brother...a mistake. The wrong man killed by the duty men. How would they explain that?

A SHIP HAS BEEN SIGHTED
in this quarter
ENGAGING IN THE UNLAWFUL ACT OF

SMUGGLING

whosoever can lay information
leading to the capture of this ship
or its crew

will receive a reward of

£500

From His Majesty's Government

This 19th day of October 1782

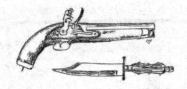

CHAPTER ONE

IT WAS A SULTRY HOT day in Canterbury. The heat beat down on the slate roof of Belcastle Manor. The cobblestone walkway was so hot that you walked in the grass if you were barefooted, as several of the servant girls were doing. The guests inside the house stood near an open window hoping for a breeze.

The ladies were busy with their jeweled fans that waved back and forth. It was the hottest day that anyone could remember. The heat did not do anything to lessen the spirits of several young men gathered at the bottom of a large staircase.

Today, May 12, 1791, was Catherine's eighteenth birthday. She was the daughter of Charles Bickford, Earl of Belcastle. That in of itself was enough to attract many would be suitors. But, in addition to that fact, Catherine was beautiful...most absolutely beautiful.

The young men came from the best bloodlines in all of England. Had there not been a rumor of war, a few equally as connected from France would have been there as well. Evidence of the upcoming war was seen in the red uniforms of the Army and the blue ones of the Navy scattered among the score or so of young men waiting for Catherine to make her appearance.

Outside the house, in the loft of the horse barn, two young men ignored the sweat that rolled off their brows and caused their shirts to stick to their skin. Phillip Bickford was the sixteen year old son of the Earl of Belcastle. His friend was Cole Buckley, the seventeen year old son of Peter Buckley, the Earl of Belcastle's stable master. The boys, so close in age, had grown up together. Phillip's mother had died in childbirth two years after Phillip was born.

The Earl had never remarried and Cole's mother, Margaret, had been as close to being Phillip's mother as any woman could be. The boys were inseparable and Phillip's teacher and tutors also taught Cole.

Cole was usually the more daring of the two boys, maybe because he was a year older. On this particular day, with the sun glaring down from the sky, several of the servant girls decided to get under the shower and cool off until they were needed again.

A place had been setup behind the barn with planks laid down on the ground and a partition built around the area to protect the modesty of those bathing. However, in the loft of the barn, a few boards were loose, allowing one to view down on those bathing below.

Meg Dawson was eighteen and she had suggested to the other servant girls to take a shower. Their uniforms and undergarments were soon slung over the privacy partition and four girls were squealing and giggling as the lukewarm water rained down on their naked bodies. The two boys, seeing the girls, looked at each other, all smiles.

Phillip, peering down, said in a loud whisper, "Look at Bess's diddleys."

"They are nice alright, but I'll take Meg's catheads any day," Cole responded. At his words, Meg looked up. If she saw the boys staring down, she didn't say anything but a slight smile flashed.

"Lord, but Molly has a set of kettle drums," Cole whispered, looking down on the large girl.

"Let me see," Phillip said, pushing a bit harder on the loose board, as he leaned to get a better look.

CRACK!!! The board broke and Phillip's upper body fell forward, causing more boards to break loose from their nails. The girls all looked up to see Phillip's upper body, with arms flung out and waving, hanging out of the loft.

Several girls screamed and reached for their clothes, while Cole was pulling desperately on Phillip's legs, finding it hard to hold him in the loose hay that covered the floor. Thankfully a hand, strong and calloused, grasped his shoulder and began pulling him and Phillip back into the loft. Both boys breathed a sigh of relief until they turned and looked into the stern face of Peter Buckley.

"It's a good thing you two were chatting away so loudly or I'd not come up to see what was so exciting."

Cole thought, *so much for being quiet*.

"Lucky for you two or you'd both have broken your necks," Peter snarled, not happy finding the boys peeping at the girls.

Cole and Phillip looked at each other, both of them thinking that a broken neck might have been preferable to what was likely to take place. As they were marched from the barn, Cole saw Meg Dawson had lingered when the other girls had dressed and ran off. Cole was sure as they went past that she gave him a wink. The wench, he thought, she'd known that they were up there all along.

CHAPTER TWO

TWO WEEKS OF CLEANING OUT horse stalls in the stable was the prescribed penance for Cole and Phillip. The end results were far less than Cole's father had hoped for. While the work was hot, dirty, and smelled to high heaven, it gave the two friends time to talk and reflect upon the delightful sights that they'd seen, and not feel the remorse Peter had hoped for. They both vowed that they'd find a way to gaze at the wonderful bodies of the opposite sex in a manner where the consequences of getting caught would be far less.

The boys had cleaned up and were discussing a trip to Canterbury. The city was noted for its cathedral but one of the grooms that worked in the stables had filled the boys' heads about a certain tavern in the city. There worked several 'willing maids' in the tavern who would provide a list of favors for six pence to a shilling, depending on the maid and the favor desired. This had the boys excited and ready to make the short ride.

The Earl, however, had other plans that the boys knew nothing about. A Navy captain had been invited to the manor. During his visit, he had set in motion the possibilities of Phillip becoming a midshipman. While sixteen was a bit old to be starting out, Captain Best assured Lord Bickford that young Phillip would be placed under a senior seaman and a trusty lieutenant until he'd caught up with all the other mids.

When the question of Cole arose, the captain hesitated, "The boy is seventeen. He would find it difficult to adjust, I believe. Phillip is almost at that age. But with your backing I don't see why a commission in the Army cannot be had. Both boys will need an allowance of say one hundred pounds so that they can hold their own with others of their position."

"It's decided then," Lord Bickford said. "Phillip will go to the Navy and Cole to the Army."

The boys appeared soon after they were called, cursing their luck and wishing that they'd left ten minutes earlier. When the boys entered Lord Bickford's office, Cole's father was already there waiting with the Earl.

The Earl started off by saying that the boys were at an age where it was time to plan for their future. The plan for Phillip becoming a midshipman and Cole becoming an officer in the Army was laid out. Both boys were far too shocked to put up any type of protest. Phillip did ask why both he and Cole couldn't be midshipmen together or join the Army together.

Peter, Cole's father, spoke up then, "If you were to both join the same service, you'd be separated at once. You'd not serve together." He continued in a much sterner voice, "You have shared a wonderful childhood, but you are no longer boys. You're young men and it's time to put away childish things, and accept the responsibility that comes with growing up."

Everyone was silent for a long moment, and then Phillip asked, "May we be excused?" His father nodded and the boys departed.

Phillip cursed, "I wish we'd never decided to look at those catheads."

"Well we did," Cole responded, and then added, "We still have time to get to Canterbury."

***

TWO BOYS RODE THEIR HORSES into Canterbury...two men rode home. They found the tavern, the Game Cock, easy enough and when the owner found out what the boys desired and had the purse to pay for their wants; two very lovely young maidens were produced. Neither one of them appeared to be over twenty but the tavern owner guaranteed that both young ladies were knowledgeable in the ways to pleasure a man.

Riding home with their sexual appetites sated, the thoughts of the changes soon to take place in their lives came to the forefront. Neither of the two could see a way to get out of the plans, Phillip in particular. Cole had a least a degree of leeway. He could visit different army barracks, as well as cavalry and dragoon units.

Phillip, on the other hand, would be joining *HMS Diamond*, a thirty-eight gun frigate. It was now in Portsmouth. In less than two months, he had to obtain the uniform and other articles needed to outfit a new midshipman. Falconer's Dictionary of the Marine and The Young Sea Officer's Sheet Anchor were two books at the top of the list of books recommended by Captain Best. All of this would be available in Portsmouth.

The trip to Portsmouth was made the following Monday. Cole accompanied Phillip and Phillip's father. Riding in the Earl's crested coach, it amazed Cole how when the coach stopped to change horses, the people all called Phillip's father, "my Lord." While he'd grown up at Belcastle and he'd always known Phillip's father was an "Earl" he'd never actually heard him addressed as Earl. It was always "my Lord." Cole knew he needed to discuss this with his father soon.

He didn't want to embarrass himself if he was to become an officer in the Army. He'd heard that the Earl's title ranked just below a Duke and Marques and a Duke was just below a Prince. Well, he had time to figure it out. Maybe he'd ask Phillip to write down the order of noble titles. Surely he would know.

***

THE TIME IN PORTSMOUTH WENT by way too fast, ending sadly with Phillip getting into a ship's boat and being taken out to *HMS Diamond*. They had all gone aboard the ship the previous day. After dining at the captain's table, Cole felt sorry for his friend and thought that maybe he was getting a better bargain.

If the captain's quarters were so small, Cole could only guess how tight and cramped the midshipman's quarters would be. Probably no larger than a horse's stall, and that was to be shared. No, he'd miss Phillip he knew, but the Navy was not for him.

There was a tremble in Phillip's voice, as they said their farewells, "Do write me, Cole." Leaning forward, he whispered, "If you tumble Meg, I want to know about it...every detail."

Cole, who had to try hard to maintain his emotions, broke out in a smile. "I shall, no worries there, I shall."

It was down the side of the ship then and back to the waiting coach. Once out of the city and headed to Canterbury, Cole spoke, "I will surely miss Phillip."

Laying his hand on Cole's knee, the Earl spoke, "So shall I, Cole, so shall I."

It was the closest that Cole had ever felt to Phillip's father.

CHAPTER THREE

T HE BUFFS WAS THE NAME the Royal East Kent Regiment went by. Cole and his father were on their way to talk to the officer in charge about a commission for Cole. A letter from the Earl was tucked inside Peter's coat. As the officer that they were to see was away, Peter spoke to his son.

"Cole, we'll not wait around like some stray dog. I'll leave word for where we can be reached, and then we'll enjoy a good lunch." Cole liked the idea.

The Boar's Head Tavern was used by Canterbury's wealthy citizens. Several of the tavern's patrons spoke to Cole's father, recognizing him as one of the Earl's two most trusted men. Frequently, the two were together.

Cole, on the other hand, had rarely been around when his father interacted with Canterbury's upper crust. At those times, he did not appreciate the standing and prestige his father was held. Was this because he was the Earl's man? What would it be like were he not the Earl's man? For some reason this bothered Cole. His train of thought was suddenly broken when a large man walked up, casting a shadow over the table.

"Angus MacFadyn, my wife's own brother!" Peter spoke to the newcomer. "What brings you to Canterbury?"

"Errands, brother-in-law, errands," Angus replied.

Cole liked Uncle Angus, who was a tavern owner in Deal. He was a loud, burly Scotsman, and the strongest man that Cole had ever known. He spoke in a strong Scottish brogue. His tavern was the Cock & Bull, a very profitable establishment. He had a sailor's widow for a cook, who was considered the best in the land. She was the best in Deal at any rate.

The tavern had been built against an existing stone cottage that was converted into four individual bedrooms for those wishing to spend the night. MacFadyn appeared well off from his dress.

Cole had once overheard his father, Peter, talking to his wife about her brother. "Aye, he has made a good living for himself. Him and every merchant in Deal when they pay no taxes on most of the articles they sell."

Cole's mother became angry and retorted, "Do you think his Lordship pays the King's tax on all the fine bottles of wine and other spirits he purchases, not to mention his tobaccos or the silk that's used to make such fine dresses for Catherine?"

Peter Buckley, wise husband that he was, changed the subject and made a hasty departure. Puffing on his pipe, he had to admit that the tobacco was fine and not so expensive that he couldn't enjoy it.

The three men were just starting to talk about obtaining Cole a commission when someone blocked the sunlight shining through the window on to their table. It was an Army officer.

"Major Huntington," the officer said, introducing himself.

"Peter Buckley," Cole's father responded, rising to shake the major's hand. "This is my son, Cole. And my brother-in-law, Angus MacFadyn."

Cole and Angus had both stood up to shake the major's hand. The major, without appearing to do so, was taking in their refined appearance as well as their manner and speech. The boy seemed familiar, but why? He appeared to be a good candidate for a commission, especially since he was recommended by the Earl with a guarantee of funds and general allowance.

The major sat down when invited and explained that Colonel Dodd was away temporarily and he was the acting commanding officer. It dawned on Huntington, after a few moments, that he did indeed recognize Cole. "Tell me, young sir, were you by chance at Catherine's birthday?"

Cole smiled, as he thought that he'd recognized the major as well. "Yes sir, Phillip and I were there. I think you were watching all the young suitors making fools of themselves, as Phillip and I were doing. I believe I recall you saying to his Lordship that Catherine was the most charming and beautiful young lady you'd ever seen."

Phillip had whispered, "By God, I think he means it." Cole didn't mention that though.

The major was a little embarrassed, when Peter spoke, "I'd have been amazed had you not thought so, Major." He then added, "And so would any other male who didn't look upon her as a sister."

The major then asked, "Pardon my asking, sir, but what is your relationship to the Earl? The letter sounded like Cole was his ward."

Peter smiled, "The Earl and I go back over twenty years. He and I served for a while in the Army, although I was not a soldier. I was responsible for acquiring horses for the Cavalry, an agent of sorts. My abilities with horses impressed Lord Bickford, so that when he became the Earl, he asked me to join him as his stable master.

Shortly after Lady Bickford died, my wife, Margaret, became Catherine and Phillip's mother, so to speak. Cole, Catherine, and Phillip grew up as playmates, but more like brothers and sister. We live in a wing at Belcastle," Peter said, anticipating the major's next question.

"I see, sir, please understand that questions are asked of all applicants."

Peter knew that having funds did not qualify a man's acceptance alone. His background was a big part of it.

Huntington then looked at Cole, "Do you enjoy horses, Cole?"

"Yes sir, I'm a good horseman, one of the best at the hunts."

By hunts, the major knew he meant fox hunts. "I must say, Mr. Buckley, I think Cole will be granted his commission with no difficulties. It may take a short time as the Buffs have a full roster of officers right now. But tell me, Cole, would you rather be an officer in the infantry or the Dragoons?"

"The Dragoons of course, sir."

The major smiled, "So would I. I have, in fact, applied for a transfer to the 10th Regiment of Dragoons. It's also known as the Prince of Wales. I've been told the transfer has been looked upon most favorably. The only problem is it's likely to be a year or so before it's official. With your permission, Cole...and yours as well, Mr. Buckley, I will amend the request to apply for the same regiment. I'm sure the request will be looked upon most favorably, as is mine. You must be patient, Cole. In the British army, things move slowly even when you have an Earl's backing."

***

PETER RODE WITH ANGUS AS they returned to Belcastle. He informed his brother-in-law of Cole and Phillip's recent incident of peeping at the servant girls bathing. He was somewhat concerned that if any further incidents arose, he might jeopardize his standing with the Earl. Phillip was gone to sea and the Earl might not feel quite so fatherly as he had when Phillip was present.

"Aye," Angus agreed. "It's a point you have, and it might be time for the boy to have to work like a man so when this commission comes along, he'll appreciate it more."

Peter turned to his brother-in-law, "My thoughts travel that same path, Angus."

When they reached Belcastle, Peter, with Cole in tow, reported to the Earl. "Splendid idea," Lord Bickford said. "I'm not sure why I didn't think of that. I know the General very well. I will send him a letter, letting him know that Cole's application will be coming and the boy has my full backing."

Cole, feeling his father's fingers dig into his shoulders, thanked the Earl and made his departure.

Peter spoke again once Cole was gone. The Earl had long ago made a point of telling Peter that when it was just the two of them, there were no formalities. When he spoke, he addressed the Earl as Charles. "Charles, I think our boys are at a point where their humours dictate their actions, and not the head on their shoulders. Phillip's humours, I'm sure, have been driven into the background being at sea. Cole's have not. Therefore until word arrives for him to depart for the army, I'm sending him to Deal to work for Margaret's brother."

The Earl knew Angus. He did, in fact, a fair amount of business with him...private business purchasing duty free products. "Do you not think that there's work for the boy here, Peter?"

"There's work, Charles, but who'd push him. They'd seek his favor by doing his work rather than push him."

The Earl nodded, "I wish that I'd known more about the yeomanry and labors when I was an officer." Charles Bickford, the Earl of Belcastle gave a sigh. "Peter, I have several requests from young men to call on Catherine and several invitations for parties. Wade through some of these with me and tell me what you hear or know of them."

Peter smiled, "Is one of them from a Major Huntington, Charles?"

"Yes, I believe so."

"Let's start with that gentleman, sir."

The Earl raised his eyebrows, "Yes, let's do that."

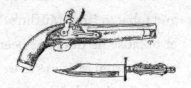

CHAPTER FOUR

ANGUS MacFADYN LEFT BELCASTLE THE next morning, with Cole on the seat beside him, after they had broken their fast.

"This trip I've a stop to make in Sandwich," Angus volunteered. "We'll be in Deal in time for the evening crowd."

"You said this trip. Do you take different routes?"

"Aye, lad, sometimes I travel to Dover and then home. Other times it is to Sandwich and home. It's little difference either way. It depends on if I have business in one place or another. A few times I've went one way going and another coming back."

"It depends on what goods you are hauling."

Angus looked at Cole, "Is that a question you are asking me, lad?" As he asked this, Angus took out his pipe and tobacco, handing the reins to Cole.

Cole paused, realizing he was on dangerous grounds. He had heard enough about smuggling to know that it was known far and wide but it was not to be discussed. Cole swallowed and spoke, "It's not a question I'd ask if another person was around, Uncle, but mother and father have mentioned his Lordship buys his spirits and tobacco from Mifflin's. He buys them there because it's cheaper because no duty has been paid on the product. Father uses the tobacco from Mifflin's as well. At one time or another, I've seen you unloading hogsheads of tobacco and barrels of spirits at Mifflin's."

Angus looked at his nephew, "It's a good head you have on your shoulders, lad. Make sure you keep it there by watching your tongue."

"I will, Uncle."

Angus punched Cole on the thigh then, "Aye, lad, I can see you're a smart one, and I've no fears of your talking where it would cause you harm. But remember, I does no talking in front of your aunt."

"I understand," Cole said with a smile. "How long does it take to travel to Deal," he asked, trying to make conversation with his uncle.

"I average about two miles an hour with the wagon loaded, and I always stop and rest the horses one or two times. Eight hours is a quick time loaded, and just pulling the wagon I can do it in five or so. I swap horses, of course, with your father each trip. If you were riding a good horse at any easy trot, you could do the trip in three hours or so."

Cole nodded his head, "If I become an officer in the Dragoons, I want to know all I can about horses."

"Aye, lad, and what better person to teach you than your own father."

***

THE SUN WAS GOING DOWN when they stopped the wagon alongside of the Cock and Bull. The sign had a fighting cock on the left side and a bull with horns on the right. Beneath the word 'tavern' was the word 'tobacconist'.

Hopping down from the wagon, Cole turned to see a beautiful young lady sitting in a landau carriage. He knew about the landau, as he and Phillip had ridden the stage to London to pick up one for the Earl. It had been a much easier ride going back to Canterbury. The girl in the landau smiled at Cole as he raised his hand in greeting. Her father had just walked out as Angus was heading to the entrance.

"Sir William, it's a pleasure to see you, sir."

Sir William smiled at Angus, "Your man had my tobacco waiting as you said, Angus. I do believe that it's the best I've ever tasted."

"Aye, and some say it's better in a clay pipe," Angus replied.

"I will try that, Angus." Sir William's eyes then took in the boy who was staring at his daughter.

Seeing the man's gaze, Angus spoke, "Sir William, this is my very own nephew, Cole Buckley. Young Cole is awaiting his commission in the Dragoons, The Prince of Wales own."

Sir William's attitude changed suddenly, "You must have some patronage for that regiment, young sir."

Angus said, before Cole could open his mouth, "Aye, that he does, Sir William. The Earl of Belcastle, no less."

Sir William nodded but didn't speak for a moment, and then as if he'd made up his mind about Cole, he spoke, "My daughter, Anne Brabham."

"My pleasure," Cole replied. "Cole Buckley at your service," he said, giving a bow. Using the best of his tutor training, he acted very much the gentleman.

"Anne has just turned sixteen," Sir William announced. "We are having a party Saturday if you'd care to come."

"It would be my honour, sir, to attend."

"Good," Sir William said and then turned, dismissing Cole and his uncle.

A servant lent a hand to Sir William as he got into the landau, closed the door and then got into his seat. Anne turned slightly, as they pulled away, to look back and give a small wave. Her father must have spoken to her, as she turned back quickly.

"Careful there, Cole. Sir William is a gentleman but were his daughter to be hurt or offended, I shouldn't want to be in that person's shoes. He is also the magistrate."

***

A BOY WITH A LIMP walked out of the tavern. Angus put his arm on the boy's shoulder and said, "Sidney, this is my nephew, Cole. He is here to help out for a while."

Sidney nodded and then asked, "Put up the wagon and team?"

"Aye," Angus said. "The wagon is empty so there's nothing to store."

Sidney nodded again and walked to the horses and wagon. Once he was out of sight, Angus leaned close to Cole. "Poor boy lost his mother and father at the same time. They were fishing and a blow came up. His parents drowned and the lad had a bad broken leg. The people who found the boat said it was awash and would have sunk at anytime. Your Aunt Florence, being the God fearing woman that she is, said we were taking him in. We've had no wean that lived so I didn't argue."

Cole knew that wean was Scottish for child, so he just shook his head in understanding. Angus spoke the King's English most of the time, so it was understood; but on occasion Cole had to ask what he meant when he used Scottish words and phrases.

He smiled as this reminded him of his uncle farting at the table once. Angus said, "Ah let wan go," before Cole's mom could speak.

The front room of the tavern had a strong tobacco smell to it. As Cole looked about, he could see a couple of shelves, one above the other, that lined two walls. Below the bottom shelf were barrels, or catheads, filled with tobacco and on the shelves were glass jars filled with more tobacco. On the far wall was a lone shelf and a stool, and that's where someone rolled cigars. Tobacco leaves hung from a wire that ran above the shelf. Below the shelf were a couple of crates with different types of tobacco.

Cole had noted that more people were starting to smoke cigars. He had tried one, but as yet he hadn't acquired the taste. Looking at all the molds on the shelf used to roll cigars at various lengths and thickness showed that the cigar business undoubtedly was picking up.

A girl was waiting on the few men there, when Angus and Cole walked into the tavern. Seeing Angus most of the men spoke. Turning to the girl, Angus asked, "Where's me bride, Peg."

"She went with the good reverend down to the orphanage," Peg replied, cutting her eyes to Cole.

"'Tis my nephew, Peg, so mind your manners when he's about."

Peg smiled and ran her fingers through Cole's hair as she took a tankard of ale to one of the men at the table.

Angus turned to Cole, "Go around back and help Sidney. I will have a piece ready when I can get Peg into the scullery." A 'piece' was a sandwich and 'scullery' was the kitchen.

I'm going to have to learn a bit more of the Scottish sayings, Cole decided.

A small stable of sorts was behind the tavern. On the right side was a lean-to coming off the wall of the stable. The opposite side was walled up as well, but both ends were open. There were two doors for the stable. One was a storage area with various objects hanging from pegs in the wall.

Seeing Cole, Sydney spoke, "This is a storage area. Sometimes when supplies come in and there's no room in the cellar, we stack them in here."

They went through the second door, with Cole following Sidney. This room was filled with horse stalls, six Cole counted, hay, an empty bin that was for corn when they had it, and buckets to tote feed and water for the horses.

"Where do you get the water from?" Cole asked.

"We have a well beside the tavern. It was a spring, but Mr. Angus dug it out and lined the sides with stone and then put a roof over it. He said he didn't like the thought of drinking water a pigeon shat in." Both boys laughed at that.

CHAPTER FIVE

JOE LANDO STOOD AMIDSHIP OF the lugger *Kestrel*. He thought the lugger was a poor ship to be named after such a graceful bird. The kestrel hawk was a hunter...a predator. The lugger was a far cry from its graceful namesake.

The captain was an older man. He had once sailed an Indiaman, but now in his eighties he was lucky to have a ship at all. The crew was small. Eight men, not including Joe, and a lubberly priest who was pale and had not moved far from the top rail that he was holding on the bulwark. Joe had greeted the man as would be appropriate for a man of God. The man nodded, acknowledging Joe's greeting. As he nodded, he heaved and leaned over the rail, casting his stomach contents into the sea. Joe immediately got upwind of the priest. Captain Raulerson just smiled.

While the lugger only had a small crew, she carried a fortune in contraband to be sold in England. Joe had delivered the money for the cargo, and not a word had passed once the introductions were made. The agent counted out the money and nodded to an underling who took Joe in tow to where the cargo was staged, waiting on the buyer to pick it up.

Joe worked for Sir George Aylward. The man had money and contacts. Most everybody knew that Sir George was the money man behind most of the smuggling in and around Deal.

Sir William Brabham was Deal's magistrate. He had done his best to catch Sir George, thinking the man an embarrassment to England. However, the two or three men who could testify against Sir George enjoyed the standard of living which he afforded them. It was a rare person that would bite the hand that fed them.

The sun was low in the sky and a gentle wind filled the lugger's sails. The priest groaned when a lookout called down, "Customs cutter coming up from astern."

Joe cursed, "Damnation. This lugger will never out sail that Customs boat."

"It'll be dark in fifteen minutes," Captain Raulerson said. "She'll not be up to us in that time." Joe hoped the old man knew what he was talking about.

BOOM...the Customs boat fired a cannon. A splash came down a hundred yards or so astern. *That was close,* Joe thought. *She doesn't have to catch us before dark, she can sink us.*

"Bring her up a point," Raulerson told the helmsman.

Another boom...the ball was closer but now it landed more to the larboard side.

"Put her back on her original course," the captain ordered. He was in effect zigzagging just before the Customs gunner fired, throwing the aim off. *How long before he catches on,* Joe wondered.

The old captain stood near the tiller watching the Customs boat. He said something to the helmsman just as a boom was heard. The ball landed close off the starboard side, drenching the priest. *If that doesn't cure his seasickness nothing will,* Joe thought. Dark was almost upon them, but so was the Customs boat.

It looks like my marriage may be postponed, if not worse, Joe thought, his mind on the beautiful Mary Stuart. His thoughts then went to the widow, Linda Eriksson. Her husband had been killed in an ambush intended for his brother. Matthew and Linda had been friends of Joe and Mary. A turn of events that he would have never expected left Matthew dead and his brother still walking.

The Customs cannon boomed again. This time a crash was heard. Joe looked and felt his heart rise up in his chest. The ball had hit where the priest was sitting. There was nothing left that could be identified as a man. *Go with God,* Joe thought to himself.

The captain saw where Joe was staring and spoke, "He was not a real priest, just a foreign agent."

Joe suddenly felt angry. Disguise was one thing, but putting on a priest's Cossack ought to be punished. It was sacrilegious. Another thought came to Joe. *He was punished by his own government. The agent didn't deserve to die that way.*

Raulerson spoke to one of the hands. The man removed a canvas covering from what looked like a stack of cargo, showing a swivel gun. The mate went about loading the gun, only he was using, in addition to ball, nails and broken glass.

"Is that necessary?" Joe asked.

"Puts the fear of God in 'em," the old captain replied.

"Who's to say they won't turn to the same tactics against us?" Joe replied.

Once the weapon was loaded, the cover was loosely placed back over the gun. The mate then shifted a few crates and hid down behind them. Joe watched as the crew took muskets, pistols, and blades and arranged them at strategic spots. The Customs boat undoubtedly had a crew twice or three times the size of the lugger.

The difference was these men were fighting for their lives, whereas the Customs men were paid a salary. If it proved to be a fight, the Customs men were not as likely to go all out. They'd prefer to go home to their wives, a good tankard of ale and a warm fire.

The cannon boomed again and the ball splashed just in front of *Kestrel's* bow. Raulerson spoke to a man and the sail was taken down.

The Customs boat pulled alongside and the captain yelled, "Why didn't you heave to?"

"Thought you might be a blackhearted sod," Raulerson replied.

Several of the Customs men were along the side of the boat. "Pass a line," someone said.

It was followed by, "We intend to board you in the name of His Majesty's Customs Service."

"Come ahead," Raulerson said.

As the Customs men made to board, the canvas was snatched off the swivel gun, which was quickly aimed and fired. The destruction was unlike anything Joe had ever seen. Where a group of men had been was now nothing but a mass of blood and gore. Musket fire broke out from both the lugger and the Customs boat. Joe ducked down as balls thudded into the deck. More than one man cried out. Someone on the lugger hoisted the sail. The wind filled it and Joe could feel it moving. A few muskets were fired at the fleeing lugger but they died out.

Joe was surprised that a cannon wasn't fired at them and then realized the men were without a leader. As Joe rose up and looked about, he saw Raulerson slumped over. His blue coat was now very dark where the man's blood oozed out.

Raulerson spoke to a mate. "Take the *Kestrel* name off the stern and chop it to kindling and toss it overboard. Anchor off the beach so that we can land our passenger and get ready to unload. Bury me at sea once we unload."

Captain Raulerson looked up and saw Joe. "A lively crossing, wouldn't you say?"

"Aye," Joe replied.

The old man nodded. "It's the way to end me final voyage."

As Joe made it ashore and was headed home, he thought maybe that was the way the old captain wanted it. At least, it was in his element. He didn't die a washed up has-been on the street.

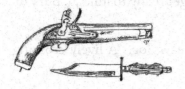

CHAPTER SIX

THE NEXT MORNING, AFTER ARRIVING at the tavern, Cole woke up and, peering out the window of his room, thought it was still night. The wind howled outside and down the hill toward the channel the rain came down in sheets. Volley after volley, almost like muskets firing on the ground of the buffs in Canterbury. One soul, braver or dumber than most, hurried forward, one hand holding his hat and the other holding his coat together trying to keep out the wind and rain. Wave after wave crashed ashore down along the beach.

The man fighting the elements pushed open the tavern door. His eyes came to focus on Cole. "Be the good doctor here, lad?"

"No sir," Cole replied quickly. He didn't know who the doctor was but the only people there were the ones who stayed there.

"Is Florence here then?"

Cole nodded and then ran to his aunt and uncle's room. Both of them were up, and Cole quickly explained, "There's a man calling for Aunt Florence."

Angus and Florence went out into the tavern. "Joseph Lando," Angus bellowed. "Are ye daft to be out in such weather?"

Lando smiled, "Were it not necessary, I'd be warming my heels beside a fire. The blacksmith asked me to find the doctor. It's time for his wife."

"Another bairn, is it? Come Florence." They bundled up and Angus put a tarpaulin around his wife. They paused at the door. "You coming, Joseph?"

Shaking his head no, Lando replied, "I've done my good deed. I didn't help with the making, so I see no reason why I should help with the bringing the child into the world."

"Humph...," Florence grunted but Angus laughed. *It was funny,* Cole thought.

"I mistook you for Sidney when I walked in," Lando said, speaking to Cole. "I can see now that you are older and taller."

"I'm Cole Buckley. Angus is my uncle. I've been sent to help out here, but in truth it was to keep me out of mischief until my commission is ready."

"Did they tell you that?"

"No, but we got caught watching the servant girls showering so it wasn't hard to figure out."

"Is it a woman's man you are?"

Cole thought on that a moment before he answered. "No, but I can think of no better pass time when I'm not busy."

Lando gave a hearty laugh. "That's two of us, lad...that's two of us."

Cole had built a fire when Sidney finally got Peg rousted out. The fire was ready so Peg started breakfast. "Will you be eating with us, Joe?"

Lando nodded his reply as he downed the last of the brandy that Cole had poured for him. "I'm starting to feel like a human again," Lando volunteered.

Peg asked if they'd rather have coffee or chocolate. Coffee was the one Lando wanted, so Cole and Sidney went along.

"Joe's a fighter," Peg informed Cole. "He's Lord Aylward's right hand man." She then added, "If he don't get caught owling."

Lando paused with his coffee cup halfway to his mouth. Cole was not sure what owling was but whatever it was, Lando didn't like it one bit.

"It's talk like that, what makes people disappear, girl," Lando remarked.

Peg gave a strained laugh, "There's naught about, Joe."

Lando didn't answer but the look he gave left Peg nervous. *Owling, it's something that I'll have to ask my uncle about...when we're alone,* Cole thought.

***

COLE SAW, LOOKING OUT HIS bedroom window, that it was a beautiful Saturday morning. *Hopefully it will get even better,* Cole thought. Today was Anne's birthday party. Cole wanted to impress Sir William so that he'd be trusted and be allowed to visit Anne at different times. He recalled the Earl speaking to Phillip and him once when they'd skipped a session on proper etiquette. 'It saddens me that the two of you would disrespect my judgment, having hired the best man I could find to teach you both the proper ways of a gentleman. Any lout can gain a title, but to be a success in life, a man must be able to conduct himself in such a manner as to bring credit to his name and that of his family.'

Cole had indeed felt bad at his actions because he truly did want to make the Earl proud of him. As his father explained, there was nothing that obligated the Earl to include Cole in all the education and benefits that he'd received along with Phillip. He'd gone on to say it was a poor man that threw away these opportunities.

Sir William's house was nice, but nowhere near the size of Belcastle. That's not to say it was not impressive in its own sort of way. One of Sir William's groomsmen took the reins of Cole's horse as he dismounted. Cole had received an engraved invitation that past Thursday. Thankfully, he'd remembered to bring it with him.

A Negro doorman in a liveried uniform stood at the door and held his hand out, "Invitation please, sir."

Smiling, Cole produced the invitation at which time the doorman opened the door, and another servant was given the invitation. He walked a few paces, with Cole in tow, and announced to the room, "Mr. Cole Buckley of Belcastle."

Anne was close by and met him as he walked down the three steps into a great room. Smiling, she took Cole's arm and led him into the room. She was wearing a gown that was more a pearl color than white. It was cut low enough that he could see the swell of her breast, but not as low as some of the ladies who attended the Earl's parties.

One brazen woman took Cole's hand and, leaning far enough over for Cole to see all of her wares, whispered, "Come see me when you turn eighteen. I'll show you things these little servant girls never thought of."

Secretly, Cole wasn't sure that he wanted to see the woman. However, Anne, who was holding his arm and standing so close that he could smell the soap and freshness of her hair, was definitely somebody he wanted to visit, to be close to and not just to taste her favors. This beautiful girl made his heart beat wildly in his chest, and seeing her almost took his breath.

Sir William broke his reverie. "It's a pleasure to see you, Master Cole."

"The pleasure is all mine, Sir William. I'm honoured to be invited to celebrate Anne's birthday. You have a beautiful and charming daughter, sir." Having seen the painting above the large fireplace, Cole knew that it had to be Anne's mother. "I can see your daughter takes after her mother, Sir William." Cole quickly realized that this had been the right thing to say.

"Her mother is a rare woman. Unfortunately, she is in London with her own mother, who is not long for this world, I fear."

"I'm sorry to hear this, Sir William. Should I be able to be of any assistance, sir, you only have to ask." Cole wondered if he'd laid it on a little too much, seeing the look on Sir William's face.

"You and every young blade here, Master Cole." Sir William then added after a pause, "But in your case, I do believe you speak from the heart."

***

THE REMAINDER OF THE DAY was like a blur. They had eaten, played games and then danced. Cole danced a few dances with Anne and some with a few of the other 'young ladies' present. When the time had passed and it was time for the last dance, Cole found Anne back as his partner. It did not sit well with the other young gentlemen and was evident by the glares he was given.

Anne whispered, after the dance, "Ask my father if you might call upon me sometimes."

Cole replied, "That I most assuredly will do."

Anne gave him a quick kiss on the cheek, which drew even more evil looks from the other male guests. Some of them even mouthed threats. Cole, however, was so thrilled and excited by Anne's affection that he ignored the others.

When the party was over and he had mounted his horse, Cole realized that he was the last guest to depart. He was so caught up in his good luck that he failed to see the boys sitting on their horses at the fork in the road. When he did see them, he knew he faced a group with malice in their hearts.

"Look what we have here," the largest of the boys said. "A knight who thinks that he can just ride in and lay claim to my girl."

Cole knew this was a situation in which no matter what was said or done, it was going to end up in a fight. What was that the fencing instructor said? "When a situation develops, don't let the other dictate the manner in which to go about it."

"Your girl is it?" Cole threw out to the one who had spoken.

"Yes," the lout replied.

"Why is it then I'm the one she kissed?" This brought laughter from the other boys until a stern look came from their friend.

"Get down off that horse and I'll show you."

"Gladly, but would you tell me who it is that's challenged me," Cole replied.

"I'm Dalton Stephenson."

"I see," Cole said jumping from his horse.

When Dalton made a show of dismounting, he never reckoned that Cole would be ready. He assumed that there'd be more talk and threats. He was wrong. A fist slammed into his face, smashing his nose with blood gushing out, as soon as he turned from his horse. Dalton hit the ground dazed. He was a big boy and a year older than Cole, and this was the first time that he'd ever been struck so hard. And he'd never been knocked down. In fact, most young men were afraid of him and backed down before it ever came to blows.

"Were I not a gentleman, I'd finish you while you are down, Mr. Dalton, but I shall allow you to rise if you wish. Remember though, there's more where that came from."

Rising to his hands and knees, Dalton rushed Cole, who side-stepped the boy and shoved his head into the dirt. Dalton got up slowly, wiping the grass from his face and mouth. His next action surprised Cole. "Seize him," he shouted to his followers.

Jumping from their horses, the boys rushed Cole. He hit the first boy with a looping right that knocked the boy down. Cole then backhanded the next boy, spinning him around. The third boy dived for his legs and held on with all his strength, while the other two boys grabbed his arms. Dalton then hit Cole in the gut, doubling him over. Steadying himself for the next blow, Cole was surprised it never fell. When he opened his eyes, Dalton was on his back in the grass and the other boys suddenly released him.

Joseph Lando stood there, "Are you all right, Cole?"

Cole, nodding his head said, "I am now that you showed up."

"I was watching from the Deal fork. I was content to let things go, as long as it was fair."

"You will be sorry you interfered," Dalton shouted.

"It's you who will be sorry when I tell your father that you and three others attacked this lad. More so when I tell him one of his biggest customers, the Earl of Belcastle, will be very unhappy when he hears of this."

"Humph."

"Humph...you say." Lando reached down and grabbed the neck of Dalton's coat. "Let's be going then to your house and tell him. I'm sure that he'll be interested to know it took four of you to whip one."

Dalton stammered, struggling to get loose, "Maybe I was wrong."

Releasing the boy's collar and shoving him toward his horse, Lando swore. "It's a hellish thing you've turned out to be, Dalton. You have more than one of the lads in Deal mad enough to lay for you one night to slit your throat or put a ball in your back." Turning to the other three, he continued, "And the same is liable to happen to anyone who is with him."

The boys swallowed hard and then looked at each other. In truth, none of them liked Dalton but all were afraid of him. They turned, as one, and rode off. Dalton climbed into his saddle and rode off as well.

"It's not really the boy's fault. His father has gotten rich off other men. Since his wife died he has no time for the boy, he just gives him money and sends him off. You are the first to stand up to him."

Lando and Cole got on their horses. "I'd say nothing about this were I you." Lando didn't say why, but Cole promised he wouldn't. Lando then paused, "I can see you've had training in regards to defending yourself like a gentleman, but it's a rare time that you'll face a gentleman, Cole. It's important that you learn to fight to win…to kill if it's called for, if you're to become an officer in the Dragoons, as I hear you are. I'll be by later to teach you a few things."

Cole was astonished, "Thank you Mr. Lando."

Lando smiled, "There's no mister to it, lad. It's Joseph to all but my friends. To them it's just plain Joe."

"Thank you then, Joe."

CHAPTER SEVEN

T HAD BEEN A WEEK since the party, when Sir William and Anne
next returned to Deal. Cole was walking up Broad Street when
he saw Anne coming from one of the shops. When he had first
walked Broad Street, Cole had been amazed at the goods in each
shop. They were quality goods and cheaper than in Canterbury. He
had, in fact, talked Daniel Thompson into putting back a pair of
matching tobacco pipes for his father and the Earl.

Anne was carrying a large parcel, which Cole quickly took from
her and placed in her landau. "Mistress Anne, what a pleasant
surprise."

Anne just looked at him. "Have you been scared off by Dalton
Stephenson?"

Cole instantly fumed and angrily he asked, "What would make
you think such a thing? I knocked him flat and gave two of his
minions a once over before I was thrown to the ground. You think
I'm scared? You just ask Joseph Lando."

"What was I to think since father has received no request to call
upon me?"

Cole swallowed and hung his head. "I...ah...well, Anne it is like this. I can hold my own against louts like Dalton." He kicked a pebble with the toe of his boot, with his head still hanging down. "It's different when you love somebody." Now that he'd admitted he loved Anne, he rushed on, "You see the tutors never taught us to write such a letter and I don't want to anger your father."

Anne lifted his chin with her hand, "You love me, Cole. You really do."

Cole looked into Anne's eyes. She was all excited now and the smile on her face melted his heart. "Of course, I do. Only a fool wouldn't. Every boy at your party was in love with you, and I more than them."

Anne looked at the groomsman in the driver seat. His head was straight ahead but she knew he was taking in every word that passed between her and Cole. She'd speak to him later.

"Father is at the Blue Post Inn having lunch with some people about a trial that's coming up. Get in and ride with me there."

Cole helped Anne get in and as he was climbing in, the driver patted the seat across from Anne. "Here, sir." Cole sat in the seat indicated.

"Oh Henry," Anne whined.

"Don't ask me to do something that will anger Sir William," Henry replied.

The Blue Post Inn was the nicest in Deal. Those who came to eat their midday meal were usually men of means. To provide privacy for her clientele, the owner, Kimberly Jordan, had partitioned off several small dining rooms. Today's meal was a business meal. The conversation was about the constable. For the conversation to remain a secret, only two other men were present besides Sir William: Captain Rodney Letchworth and his sergeant, Sean Duncannon. Captain Letchworth was in command of his Majesty's

Preventive Service. Neither Sir William nor the good captain were sure that the constable was a man to be trusted, hence his absence from the meeting.

All of the men knew that Sir George Aylward was the head of most of the smuggling in Deal and along the coast to Sandwich to the north, and Dover to the south. But knowing and proving it were two different things. He had affluence and he had made money. He had also lined the purses of a majority of people in the three cities. It wasn't from him personally, but through a series of agents. Was the constable one whose purse had been stuffed? If not the constable, then possibly his men. Every lead that they'd gotten turned out to be a wild goose chase. If people were actually caught, they were usually poor fishermen who were desperate to feed their families.

Captain Letchworth said he had a few of his men that could possibly find out if the constable or his men were on Aylward's list of paid men. Sir William nodded. It was a start. The captain, having nothing further to discuss, left with his sergeant in tow.

Sir William paused to speak to Mrs. Jordon. She was a quiet, refined lady. One whom Sir William would certainly be interested in, were he not a married man.

Cole was standing beside the landau when Sir William walked out. He was neither surprised nor dismayed to see the young man. He was sure Anne's need to shop was, in all honesty, a ploy to see Cole. She was smitten by the young man and that did not surprise him either.

Cole was a touch over average height, and had blonde hair. He had eyes that seem to sparkle and a firm chiseled jaw. His shoulders were wide and his muscles in his upper arm strained at the cloth in his shirt. He was polite, well educated, and had an Earl's backing. Cole was a suitable young man, Sir William had to admit.

Sir William's man had informed him about how Dalton Stephenson had laid in wait and Cole had not shown the least amount of fear, and had indeed taken the fight to the bully.

Anne was still only sixteen though, and this was something to discuss with her mother, Mary, when she returned home.

A thought struck Sir William. Greeting Cole, he mentioned a hunt was coming up soon. He'd be glad to have Cole as a guest.

"Oh, thank you, sir. I will check with my uncle and if he has nothing planned for me, I'd love to attend."

Anne's father liked the boy's response. A good many would have accepted the invitation right off. Cole knew that he had obligations that he needed to check on first. *Shows maturity*, Sir William thought.

"We are headed to your uncle's now. I'm in need of some tobacco, so we shall ask him then."

***

Leif Eriksson sat at a table toward the back of the taproom. Joe Lando was seated with him. Eriksson owned several fishing boats, but most people knew that their real job was as crafts for smugglers.

Beer and ale flowed freely, keeping Peg, and another servant girl named Betsy, running. Angus and Cole were constantly filling tankards as order after order for more spirits nearly overwhelmed the two. Both of the serving girls showed far more than the usual amount of cleavage, which helped with their tips. A ready smile and giggle didn't hurt either.

Peg came over with a tray full of tankards asking for a refill of ale all around. "There must be a meeting later tonight for all these louts to be about. One man said the taverns on Alfred Square are so full that a man can't squeeze through the door."

"What kind of meeting?" Cole asked innocently.

"To tell when the ships are coming in," Peg quipped.

"Watch your tongue, Peg, or one day you'll lose it," Angus growled. Seeing Cole's look, Angus spoke to his nephew, "We'll talk later."

CHAPTER EIGHT

THE TAVERN WAS CLOSED AND all the lights were out, not only in the Cock and Bull, but throughout Deal. Cole's uncle had taken his nephew aside and explained how a large part of Deal's livelihood came from smuggling. It was for some individuals their entire means of income. Angus explained how Parliament had put such a high tax on many items that most ordinary people couldn't afford tobacco, spirits, and even tea.

Angus looked at Cole and continued, "Therefore, for many, the only way to enjoy these items is to buy smuggled goods. All along the coast of Kent smuggling is common. Everyone knows it's going on, but nobody talks about it...nobody but a fool. The supplies landed here are sold all the way to London."

"And Canterbury," Cole threw out.

"Aye, me boy, but let's say no more about it."

"One question, Uncle, is smugglers owlers?"

"Aye!"

Why?" Cole inquired.

"When do you see owls out, lad?"

"At night."

"Aye, right you are. And when did the smugglers leave out?"

"Tonight late."

"There ye have it, they are owlers. They like to do their deeds when it's black as the Earl of Hells waistcoat." Seeing Cole's blank look, Angus added, "That means it's pitch black." Angus then went to bed.

Cole, hearing a noise and voices outside, peeped out from the curtain over the window.

Sidney, hearing Cole stir, quietly entered his room. He laid his hand on Cole's shoulder, causing him to jump. "I didn't mean to scare you," he whispered. "We are not supposed to look out the windows when the owlers are out."

Cole nodded; he was still trying to figure out how a boy with a limp was able to come up on him without his hearing. True, he'd been looking out the window, but his mind had been drifting. He'd thought about Phillip and wondered how he was doing on a ship. He'd also thought of their trip into Canterbury for a bit of mutton, as his father's stable hands called it. And Meg Dawson. He was sure that she'd known they were watching and put on a show for them.

It was different looking upon Anne. He thought of Meg with a lust in his loins. There was tightness in his chest with Anne. His heart beat fast. Was it love? He had told Anne that he loved her but did he really? Did he even know what love was? He certainly knew there was a very big difference between his lust for Meg and how he felt about Anne. He'd talk to Joe about it since he couldn't talk to Phillip.

***

SLEEP CAME AT SOME POINT, but Cole wasn't sure when. He woke up not only to sunlight in his room but to the smell of breakfast drifting into his room. He quickly dressed and rushed into the taproom where the family had breakfast.

"Did you get the cobwebs clear?" Sidney asked.

"Aye," Cole said, mimicking his uncle. "A splash of cold water did the trick and the smell of breakfast had me rushing."

"It's about time," Florence said. "I thought you intended to sleep the morning away." As she said this, Florence gave Cole a big hug.

When breakfast was over, Cole and Sidney followed Angus out back. There were a couple of barrels of brandy, one of wine, two hogsheads of tobacco, and two crates. This was the noise that Cole had heard last night. The owlers had delivered goods to his uncle. Going into the storeroom, they moved out a few barrels to move last night's supplies to the rear of the storeroom; all except the two crates. Sidney and Cole took these into his aunt and uncle's family quarters. Angus picked up one of the hogsheads and carried it through the taproom to where he kept his tobacco. He then pulled an empty container out and placed the tobacco in it.

Sidney leaned over and whispered, "That one has the King's tax stamp on it. You have to buy taxed goods now and again to keep the Customs officer happy." Cole nodded his understanding.

The work was finished in an hour's time. Peg and Betsy came in and started cleaning up what had been left undone from last night. Betsy was a new girl who had moved in with Peg. Peg had asked Angus to hire the girl so he did, but today was her first full day.

It was late in the morning when Joe Lando stopped in front of the tavern. "I have to go pick up a team of horses and farming equipment from Stuart, Angus. Would you lend me Cole for a couple of hours?"

Angus looked at Joe, the two passing unspoken words. Cole later found out that his uncle was making sure they were not hauling smuggled goods.

The road soon turned into nothing more than a cart track. John Stuart was a farmer. He was, in fact, the largest farmer around Deal. He owned a good bit of land but he also rented land from Sir George Aylward. John had a daughter, Mary, who Joe was very fond of. A rare beauty was how Joe described her.

Joe's plan was that when he'd put back a goodly amount, he planned to marry Mary. Cole, who was keen on the subject of women, talked to Joe about his thoughts last evening. Joe pulled the wagon to a stop and looked at Cole.

"I take it we are friends, Cole, and friends sometimes talk about things that stay between them."

"Aye," Cole agreed. "That's how it was between Phillip and I."

"Good, so you know what I'm talking about. Well, Cole, there's times when a man's humours get so that he's ready to boil. Its times like that that you wish for a girl like Peg, Betsy, or maybe your Meg Dawson. But, when a man is ready to marry and have a family, that's when he looks to a girl like your Anne or my Mary. Now that's not something the vicar at St. George's church would agree with, but we are talking about the realities of life man to man."

Cole dwelled on this a bit and was about to say something when Joe spoke again. "Climb down and get the gate will you, Cole."

John Stuart was an average size man but with thick arms and broad shoulders. It was apparent that he was a working man. He and Joe passed pleasantries and then Joe introduced Cole. John Stuart greeted Cole, and then said, "The team is in the stable and the plow is over there."

Looking at the plow, Cole thought, *it is no wonder he asked me to come along.* The plow was loaded and the horses were tied to the back of the wagon when Mary came out and waved.

"Come in for a bit of tea," John said to Joe. "You too, Cole."

The Stuart house was larger than it looked from the outside. It was very neat and the furnishing was better than Cole expected, but this was Deal. Mary, after a few minutes, mentioned that her cat had kittens so she and Joe walked off. Mary's father continued sitting at the table, so Cole decided to follow suit.

●●●

COLE RODE ALONGSIDE JOE ON one of the horses that they were taking to Aylward's place. Joe seemed cheerful to the point he sang a few jingles.

"Things must have gone well with Mary," Cole volunteered.

Joe's smile was all the answer needed. Neither one of them spoke while Joe packed his pipe. A breeze was blowing so it took a couple of attempts with cupped hands to get the pipe lit. Once it was lit and Joe had smoke billowing up around his head, Cole nudged closer to the wagon.

"Joe, the pact that we made talking about women, does that go for everything?" he asked.

Joe looked at Cole but didn't answer immediately. After taking a few puffs, he looked at Cole, "Aye, lad that goes for everything. But remember this, if some things are repeated it could cause a person to die. Me as well as you. You understand that, don't you?"

Cole nodded but couldn't find his voice for a minute. Finally after clearing his throat and getting up his nerve he asked, "Are you an owler, Joe?"

A large smile creased Joe's face, "Would it bother you if I was?"

Cole quickly shook his head, "No, we are friends."

"It's like this: I get the men...and some women, together to carry supplies ashore to wagons and carts to be taken to different storage places. I will occasionally ride along with a wagon."

"Aren't you afraid that you'll get caught?"

"There's risk in everything, Cole. That horse you are riding could stumble, causing you to fall off and break your neck. A fisherman risks his life every time he goes out. The reward is worth the risk."

"Reward?" Cole asked. "What type of reward?"

"Ten shillings a night for tubmen." Before Cole could ask the obvious, Joe told him that tubmen are those hearty men, and a few women, who put barrels into tubs tied over their shoulders and take them up from the beach to wagons waiting on the road. Joe continued, "Tubmen are protected by batmen. The tubmen take contraband from where it's landed to waiting wagons or pack horses. Batmen protect them if they happen upon the odd riding officer or duty man."

"How do you get tubmen?" Cole asked.

Joe laughed, "Word gets out rather quickly. Forty men for a small shipment and I have seen upward to a hundred on some nights."

"That's a lot of horses," Cole said.

"Aye," Joe agreed. "They are borrowed from local farmers and landowners. The arrangement is a cozy bargain. A keg of the best brandy is waiting on the horse owner's porch the next morning, or some money in a milk churn."

"Who gets to be a tubman?" Cole asked.

"Anybody who can keep their mouth shut. A new man is usually recommended by one of the regulars or a father with a strapping son. Farm hands, bakers, blacksmiths, fishermen are also used. A few clerks even, but they are used elsewhere mostly. We even had a parson for a few years."

Cole said, seeing the town of Deal coming into sight, "Some men came to Uncle Angus's last night. They left things that we had to put away."

"Aye, some of it's done that way, while others are put in locations for storage until it can be taken to where it is to be sold. Some goes to Canterbury where you live but most of it goes to London. Sometimes, some of it is taken by ship to other places."

Joe then pulled up on the reins to stop the horses. He knocked the ash from his pipe and looked sternly at Cole. "We've had a general conversation about the free trade. I meant what I said...loose lips could get a man killed very quickly. Also, Cole, while everyone knows, it's an ill-kept secret and it is a hanging offense. Especially if things go wrong and somebody gets killed."

Cole swallowed hard. "I heard what you said to Peg, and I've heard Uncle Angus tell her to keep her mouth shut."

Joe nodded, "One day she'll talk too much and someone will find her down by the beach dead."

Cole looked into Joe's eyes, "I'll not talk, Joe."

"I never thought that you would, Cole. Otherwise, you'd not have made this trip with me."

Cole smiled, "Thank you, Joe."

"No need to be thanking me, lad. We'll get together soon to teach you the real way to fight. I don't want it said that he died because Joseph Lando didn't do a proper job. I'll teach you about knives as well. See that tree there, Cole?"

Cole heard a thud as he turned to look. A knife was sticking dead center of a tree no bigger around than his head...and thrown from a moving wagon at about twenty to twenty-five feet.

"Damn Joe," Cole cursed with surprise and disbelief. "That's something."

"It has come in handy," Joe replied.

Cole got down at the Cock and Bull and tied his horse at the back of the wagon along side of the other horse. Joe waved good-bye and drove off in the wagon. Cole's mind was running wild with all the things he'd learned today.

Aunt Florence saw Cole and called to him. "Did you have a good day?"

"Yes, Aunt. Mary Stuart is a very pretty woman and her cat has baby kittens."

Peg glared at him. *Was she in love with Joe,* he wondered, *probably so.* She might warm Joe's bed for a night but it'd be Mary Stuart whom Joe married, Cole knew.

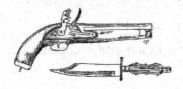

CHAPTER NINE

HAT STARTED OFF AS A beautiful day for a fox hunt soon changed. Cole walked with Anne through the stables looking at the horses that they were to ride. Anne was to ride a dapple gray mare, whom Cole thought a tall horse for a mare. His horse was a chestnut gelding, who Anne proclaimed that outside of Father's horse was the best jumper in the stable. The smell of leather and saddle soap permeated the stable. The hunting officials walked about in their pinks. Cole thought that a funny term for the officials; their jackets were as red as an Army officers. They wore white britches and high black leather boots.

Cole wore a tan tweed jacket, white britches, black boots, and a black stock tie. Anne was wearing a blue riding habit. She wore a close fitting jacket over her frilly blouse. The tight jacket punctuated her breasts every time she took a deep breath. She also wore a frilly blue cravat to match the habit, and a black top hat held in place by hair pins.

They had not noticed the color of the sky, being deep in the stable, until they'd walked toward the large open stable door. It had grown dark outside.

One of the officials remarked to his companion, "They'll not run today."

The fox hounds were off to the left in a kennel. Several of them were baying in excitement with all the activity that marked a hunt for them. A distant rumble of thunder quieted them down.

A loud crack and a flash of lightning filled the sky. It was close and frightened Anne as she grasped Cole's arm. He patted her arm and whispered, "I have you, love." Anne squeezed his arm and then turned to face him. A stable hand, with his jacket darkened where the rain drops had hit it, walked in leading a horse just as Cole and Anne kissed.

He said, in a low voice, "Sir William is coming this way, Mz. Anne."

When Sir William and a couple of friends entered the stable, Cole and Anne were leaning over the stall gate talking about her mare. Sir William looked at the two of them, and looked at his friend and then back to his daughter and Cole.

The tavern boy, Sidney, had delivered a well written letter, just yesterday, requesting that he, Cole, be allowed to visit Anne in a manner that suited Sir William and Lady Brabham.

"Excuse me, gentlemen, I have a need to speak with my daughter." He did not add "and her friend."

Cole straightened, seeing Anne's father, almost like a soldier standing at attention. Extending his hand, he spoke, "As Mother Nature has not seen fit to provide us weather for the hunt, Anne was showing me her mare."

"Do you like her, Cole?"

Cole, at first, wasn't sure if Sir William meant the horse or Anne. Anybody could see he liked Anne, so Cole figured he was talking about the horse. "She is a beautiful horse, Sir William. A bit tall for a lady, I would have imagined, but if the lady is a fine horsewoman this mare will lead the pack."

"She has the features and looks of an Arabian," Sir William said.

"Yes sir, I like her. She is a magnificent animal."

"I see your father has trained you well."

"Thank you, sir. We have three Arabian stallions at Belcastle. Some have been cross bred to some of our larger mares. Father and the Earl want to see if they can improve the quality of our other stock. He also has six Arabian mares whose bloodlines have and will remain pure."

Anne was looking at her father and Cole discussing the horses; maybe a common ground.

"Anne...Anne..."

"Ah...yes."

"Did you know that the Arabian is the oldest pure bred of horses in the world. The Arabs, in fact, are so fond of the horses that they bring them in their tents. Foals are raised alongside their children." Cole now had Sir William's interest.

"I did not know that, Cole."

"Yes sir. Father has a book on the horses by a man who lived several years with a tribe of Arabs to learn of the beautiful horses. They are not fast out of the gate but they can run forever. They're the best endurance horses in the world. It's been a dream of Phillip's and mine to raise Arabians, when I marry and settle down."

"Good," Sir William replied. "I wish you well."

Sir William and his friends left the stable leaving Cole and Anne standing by the mare's stall.

"I think you impressed my father," Anne said.

"He didn't say much," Cole replied.

"No, he didn't," Anne said. "Your comments have made him think."

"He didn't speak on my request."

"Give him time," Anne replied, laying her hand on top of Cole's.

Cole, looking around the stable and seeing no one, gave Anne a long kiss on the lips. When the kiss broke, Anne's face was flushed.

"My God, Cole, you set me on fire."

"I'm...I'm sorry."

"No, you're not," Anne said, grabbing the back of Cole's head and pulling him to her waiting and wanting lips.

The stable boy who'd seen them before took a deep breath. He'd dreamed of doing that same thing to Anne, but he was only thirteen. He backed out of the stable door and started singing. When he re-entered, Cole and Anne were walking toward the door. He threw up his hand as he passed them. Anne had a red face. Hopefully, it would clear up before they got to the house. Sir William would be hard to live with if it didn't. Making a decision, he called after the couple.

"I'd splash some cool water on my face before I go in," he offered.

Anne's hands went to her face. She touched the stable boy's arm and said, "Thank you." To Cole she said, "You rogue. Father will never allow you to visit if he sees me like this."

They stopped at the well, drew out a fresh bucket, with Anne placing a handkerchief in the cool water. She pressed the cool cloth to her face. The flush soon went away. Lunch was served and Cole left after a meal that had him wondering if he'd be able to climb up on his horse.

***

SEVERAL DAYS HAD PASSED SINCE Cole had seen Anne. He wanted to see her in the worst way but was worried that as passionate as they'd been, they might go too far. He was starting to understand what Joe meant about pent up humours. If Peg were a little more on the discreet side, he'd have taken her up on her not too subtle offers.

A little after sundown, the tavern started filling up with a more boisterous crowd than usual. He'd had some extra time that afternoon and decided to walk down Middle Street toward Alfred Square. It was in that area that some of the more daring women live, Sidney had mentioned once. Since his last visit, Cole felt like his humours were near the boiling over point. He'd not found the nerve to ask a promising lass though. She'd flirted and then laughed when he walked on by, but she was obviously a trollop. Cole certainly didn't want to catch anything.

Joe came in and sat down at a table. Peg drew a tankard of ale and took it to Joe. He smiled but waved her off. "Haven't the time, lass."

Cole, seeing Joe break out his pipe, lit a long splinter of wood and took it to him.

"Thank you," Joe said, puffing away at his pipe. Once the pipe was lit and Joe took a pull on his ale and the two chatted for awhile. Joe said, after a few minutes, "You'll have to excuse me for a while, Cole. I've business to attend to."

Cole stood up and, seeing the tall figure of Leif Eriksson, he knew his thoughts were right. There was to be a ship tonight. Thinking of the ten shillings it would bring, Cole wondered if he could sneak out. Joe would vouch for him and he was strong. The trouble was getting out, and his uncle would never agree to it if asked.

***

IT WAS AFTER MIDNIGHT AND Cole was trying to decide whether to find that girl on Middle Street or let Peg relieve his humours. Outside he heard voices...angry voices. Voices that increased to shouted curses. It came to Cole suddenly— one of those voices was Joe. Was he in a fight? Did he need help?

BANG!!! A pistol went off.

"That'll fix the bugger," a voice said. It wasn't Joe's voice. He must have been shot.

Cole had never taken off his britches, so out of his room and down the hall to the rear entrance he ran. Cole ran as silently and as fast as he could out of the back door. He'd not gone a block when he saw Joe trying to rise up off the street.

One of the men was leveling his pistol at Joe. Cole, with no weapon, charged the man, plowing into him with such a force that the villain hit the street. The jar caused him to drop the gun. The other of the two men came at Cole with a club and a knife. Cole rolled as the man swung and missed with the club. As Cole rolled, he went over the pistol. The man with the club gained his balance and was coming after Cole again. Snatching up the pistol, Cole aimed and fired.

There was a spark and loud bang. The man grabbed his chest and sunk down to his knees. The man's dingy shirt turned crimson and blood ran from between his fingers. The man, watching his life's blood ooze out of his body, looked at Joe. Almost in a whisper he said, "Blarney, Joe, I'm dead." Falling down, his head hit the street and he looked like a man praying.

Cole threw the pistol down and went to Joe. "Where are you hit?"

"My shoulder."

Voices of men could be heard coming their way. Cole helped Joe to his feet and, grabbing his hat, they moved into the shadows and over to the tavern. There were no lights in the tavern and, entering through the back door that Cole had left from, they entered and went to Cole's room.

Cole could see the wound after taking off Joe's shirt. "You must have been standing sideways," he said. "You have a deep furrow or a groove but the ball didn't go inside of you." Sneaking into the taproom, Cole got a fresh towel and a glass of brandy, and went back to take care of Joe.

Joe grimaced as the wound was cleaned and bound up. "It's lucky for me that you came when you did," Joe said. "But charging an armed man without a weapon is not the smartest thing a man should do."

"I couldn't let him shoot you, Joe."

"No, I'm glad you showed up, but killing a man can lay heavy on a man's soul."

"This won't," Cole replied. "Somebody was going to die...you, me, or him. I decided that it would be him."

Joe nodded, "We'll speak no more on it then."

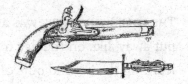

CHAPTER TEN

WHEN COLE WOKE UP JOE was gone. Joe had been on Cole's bed and he had been in a chair propped back against the wall. Cole quickly went to the side of the bed. Joe had cleaned up the bloody rags that Cole had used on the wound. Pulling back the blanket, there was no blood on the sheets either...but there was blood on his hands. Pouring water into a washbowl, Cole washed his hands and arms. He then took off the clothes that he'd worn last night and put on clean ones. He combed his hair, put on his shoes and threw the pan of bloodstained water out the window.

They were talking about the shooting once he got to the kitchen. "Two men dead, one with a broken neck and one shot in the breast. The constable thinks the one man shot the other but he got a lick in with his club before he died."

Peg looked at Cole, "Some think maybe there was three or four of them. There are tracks of a barefoot person."

Angus looked at the girl. "There's tracks all over the street, girl. How do you make out one set from another one on a busy street?"

Cole said nothing but he was sure that Peg knew more than she was saying. He'd have to let Joe know.

***

THE FOLLOWING WEEK WAS A busy one. Stores had to be rotated and put away, like on the day following the previous landing. Cole was learning the ins and outs of the tavern and Angus had hinted that he wanted to make a trip to London. He had asked Cole if he felt like he could run the tavern. Cole immediately said yes, feeling that he'd earned his uncle's respect.

He was helping with the books and pointed out that his uncle had claimed he'd sold four barrels of taxed brandy but only had an invoice to show one barrel purchased. It was similar with the tobacco but not to as large a degree.

"While I'm gone, I'll be taking care of the taxed brandy and barrel."

Cole then found out that empty barrels and hogsheads with the duty stamp could be purchased for the price of the stamp and a few shillings to the agent if you knew the right one.

Sir William had come to town to buy tobacco once before. Anne was with him. Cole wondered how a man could smoke so much, but his uncle later pointed out he was sure that Sir William gave his overseer and his head groomsman tobacco. When friends dropped by they were sure to be given a bowl along with their brandy also.

Sir William talked about the recent homicide on this trip. He told Angus that from all accounts, both men were no accounts who were lucky to be trusted as tubmen with even the smugglers. He continued on, "The constable has not been able to find one shred of evidence that anyone else was involved but I'm not sure I agree that the one who was shot was able to brain the other before he died. But regardless, murder in the streets of Deal is not to be tolerated. It's enough for the owlers to bring in contraband..." Sir William said this, hefting his bag of tobacco. "Violence will bring down the preventive service people, and the Customs agents. As magistrate,

I prefer to keep things in Deal quiet. I don't want the King's agents breathing down our necks like in Cornwall and Hastings."

Cole slipped out of the tavern at that point so that he could talk with Anne. "Mother is coming home now," she said, "so father should respond to your request to call on me, Cole."

"I hope so," Cole said, "I'm dying to see you."

"And I you," Anne replied, placing her hand on top of Cole's, which was resting on the carriage door.

The horses stamped their feet and seemed to want to move along, but Cole didn't want Anne to ever leave. They heard a noise coming from Beach Street. It was Dalton and some street urchin.

"Since you thrashed Dalton, the other boys no longer seem to be afraid of him. He pays some of the poor boys to travel along with him and do his bidding."

"You are well informed," Cole remarked.

Anne looked at Cole, "I can and do visit with other girls, you know."

Cole hadn't even thought of that but said, "I'm glad, we need to have friends." He meant this, as there was rarely a day that he didn't think of Phillip.

Sir William came out at that time. He spoke to Cole and invited him to come out to the house on Sunday. "Wear your riding clothes," he added. Cole was elated.

Sir William added, before they drove off, "I've already spoken to your uncle."

"Thank you, sir. I'd be delighted."

The carriage was pulling away when Cole noticed Dalton was almost to the tavern. For some reason, it came over Cole to greet the boy. He walked over and stuck out his hand.

"How are you today?" Dalton took the offered hand automatically and shook it.

"Would you care for a pint of small beer?" Cole asked.

Dalton looked bewildered for a moment and then smiled. "I've a thirst alright." So he followed Cole inside.

They talked on anything that came to mind for the next half hour, while the boy with Dalton sipped on tea. It was probably the best that he'd ever had. Uncle Angus called on Cole so the two boys said good-bye.

Dalton paused before he left. "I'm sorry about the fight, Cole."

"Think nothing of it," Cole replied. "We are friends now." Dalton left with a smile.

When Cole went to find his uncle, he was informed the trip to London had been decided on. They would leave the next day and he planned to take Florence and Sidney.

"Think you can handle it?"

Cole smiled and said, "Aye, Uncle. Things will be just as you do them." His uncle smiled.

It occurred to Cole that he was alone with his uncle so maybe it was a good time to have a man-to-man talk. "Uncle, you know that I see Sir William's daughter." His uncle nodded his head. Cole continued, "She has me humours boiling and I'd not touch her like that but there's others who seem willing."

Angus looked at his nephew, "Have you had a woman, Cole?"

"Aye, in Canterbury."

His uncle nodded again, "I've seen Peg flaunt her wares in front of you, so I'm surprised you've not bedded her. Keep in mind though, Cole, you'd not be the first. Go see Doctor Garrett and tell him that I sent you to get a sheepskin cundrum. It will cost you a bit."

Angus, saying this, took out his purse and gave Cole a crown and a guinea. "Say nothing of this around your mum or your aunt, understand."

Cole nodded, "They cost that much, Uncle?"

"No, but you may need a bit if you decide on some wench besides Peg. I'll not tell you to not bed Peg, but if you do, you'll be reminded of it often. I'd not want to lose the lass but if it comes to it you are more important." Cole nodded. "Off to Doctor Garrett's with ye now."

***

COLE WAS RETURNING FROM THE doctor's office when he ran up on Joe. They talked a bit and when he told Joe about Peg's innuendo, Joe got angry.

"I agree with Angus. I'd not want you to bed the wench. I have a woman in mind so let Peg know you've no interest in her."

"Don't we have to be careful that she'll talk of the murder?"

"It wasn't murder, it was self defense, and if I have to I'll go to the constable and tell him they tried to rob me and I did away with the two of them. If you are mentioned, I'll say you heard the shots and come to see what was going on. You helped me up and we both left."

"I don't mind saying that I shot the rogue, Joe. It was in self defense, like you say."

"No, lad, you've got a future. I don't want your name involved." Cole nodded his head.

Joe went to a table in the taproom, at the tavern, and Cole went to put up his purchases. When the tavern closed that night, Cole went to his room. He was tired and looked forward to his bed and a good night's rest. His aunt and uncle would leave tomorrow for London and he, Cole Buckley, would be in charge of the Cock and Bull. The weight of the responsibility suddenly seemed heavy. He'd do his best not to let his uncle down. That was no error.

When he opened the door to his room, he caught the sweet odor of perfume. A woman sat on the edge of his bed, and as he entered and closed the door the shawl she had around her slipped to the floor.

"I'm Linda. Joe said you were a man who needed a real woman, not some tavern wench."

Cole nodded but couldn't speak.

"Let me help you out of those clothes," she said.

Cole stood there as Linda undressed him, and suddenly he wasn't so tired anymore.

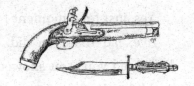

CHAPTER ELEVEN

THE NEXT DAY WAS A busy one, yet Cole felt like he was floating on clouds most of the day even though it had been the wee hours when Linda left and he fell into a contented sleep. He was dragging though by the end of the evening.

Two men got into a disagreement. One pushed the other over a table, and that man pulled a knife. Cole came from behind the bar with a club that his uncle kept for such occasions.

"Break it up or out ye go," Cole growled.

"And if we don't?"

Cole didn't talk; his answer was a club to the drunkard's head. The other man sobered quickly. "Ye didn't have to do that."

"He challenged me," Cole said. "Do you want the same?" Cole didn't know it but Joe stood up behind him.

The man, seeing Joe, lost all interest. He went over and picked up the man he'd been fighting with and walked out.

"They are brothers-in-law," Joe said.

"But it doesn't mean that they wouldn't kill each other when drunk." Now that it was all over, Cole felt nervous and weak.

"Sit down here, Cole. Are you okay?"

"Yes, just for a moment I was dizzy. Did I do right, Joe?"

"Aye, lad that you did. It was alcohol talking but the man challenged you. You showed him in front of everybody that you wouldn't tolerate insolence or allow the tavern wrecked by drunken louts. The word will get around. You better not challenge Cole Buckley if you want to keep yer teeth. It's what Angus would have done."

"Nobody has challenged him since I've been here."

"Aye, Cole, and for the same reason. Your uncle will speak once. After that...well, it's their funeral."

Linda came again that night to visit again.

"Tell Joe that I said thank you."

Linda paused, "The first night was because of Joe. Tonight was because I wanted more."

"Thank you then," Cole said. Linda smiled.

Cole stood up as a thought came to him. "I've got money."

Linda smiled again, "You are sweet, Cole, but I'm not a prostitute."

***

THE NEXT TWO DAYS FLEW by and then on Friday night Eriksson came in and took his table. *Another landing tonight*, Cole thought. When Joe came in and went to sit with Eriksson, Cole was sure of it. Things went along as usual for such a night. Peg and Betsy were busy dodging men trying to slap or pinch their rumps and trying to get a peek at their bosoms. Cole was locking up at midnight and headed to bed when a knock came at his door.

It was Joe standing there. "I need your help, Cole."

"How so?"

"One of my wagon drivers drank too much. He fell trying to climb into the wagon, breaking his arm. I need a man I can trust to drive it."

Cole agreed without thinking of the possible consequences. He put on a coat and hat and followed Joe to the cliffs. Below on the beach, men were unloading boats and starting up the hill to the waiting wagons. By the time the first man made it up the hill, a man with papers in his hands looked at what the man was carrying and directed him to a wagon. The man then went down the hill for another load. When a man was directed to his wagon, Cole saw that he carried two barrels slung across his shoulders.

There were more men standing just beyond the wagons. They carried muskets and had pistols in their belts. Cole guessed that these men must be batmen although he didn't see a club among them. Seeing how heavily armed they were, he knew that he'd involved himself in a deadly business. He trusted Joe though. If he thought the duty men would be out he'd not have called on him. But...how could he be sure. He couldn't. Seeing the number of men carrying goods and the number of wagons this was undoubtedly a big haul. Needing such a large number of men couldn't go unnoticed by the authorities...could it? Were they paid to not notice?

When his wagon was loaded Joe came up. "You remember the way to my Mary's."

"Aye."

"Go there. There is a place in the barn for the wagon. Can you back up a team?" Cole nodded yes. "Back the wagon in, unhitch the team, put the harnesses on a rack, turn the horses loose in the paddock and then leave. A horse will be in the stable stall. If a riding officer comes by, you tell him that you're coming back from a visit to the widow."

"Who is the widow if they ask?"

Joe smiled at Cole. "Linda." Cole smiled now. "You say that and it's unlikely anything else will be said. If so, you tell them who you are and that you were sent to work with Angus while you are waiting on your commission. It won't hurt to drop Sir William's name," Joe said. "But tell them that if they decide to check to be discreet as you have it in mind to call upon Anne."

Cole nodded and then clicked at the horses, slapping the reins. The horses moved at an easy gait and Cole was wishing he'd brought a cigar. It would make the night pass. He started to sing a little tune he'd learned and then stopped abruptly. Joe's instructions and recommendation were all well and good for the ride back. Was it up to him to decide what to do if he got caught going to the Stuarts'. Damned if this didn't have the possibility of turning into a hellish mess. Cole's nerves were on edge until he had the wagon parked, the horses turned out, the harnesses put up and a barrel of brandy just to the right of the barn door. The horse Cole was to ride was already saddled. He had to tighten the cinch, and then putting his foot in the stirrup he swung up into the saddle. His knee touched a bulky object and, running his hand over the object, Cole realized it was a saddle gun. Was it put there for him? *Not likely*, Cole thought after a few moments. It had to be for the original driver. He must have been a known smuggler. A story such as visiting the widow wouldn't work with him obviously. The gun meant that he'd put up a fight.

Cole felt the gravity of hauling smuggled goods come down on him. He wasn't afraid but he began to understand this was not just some game to take lightly. This was still on his mind when he came on the small road to the widow's house. Why not make a stop? Cole headed down the path, and just before he rounded a curve he heard a wagon coming. Quickly, he got the horse off the road and into the trees. He dismounted and put his hands over the horse's mouth to keep it from whinnying at whoever it was passing by.

It was only a moment until the wagon went by. Actually it was a small one horse carriage or buggy. It was Doctor Garrett. *Humm, wonder if he uses his own lambskins*, Cole thought. Debating on whether to ride on or not, a barking dog settled it for him. He rode up to the house.

Linda stood at a side door with a lantern. "Who's there?"

"Linda, it's me, Cole."

"Well, get down and come in," she said.

Cole apologized as he went up the steps, "I didn't mean to come in so late but thought I'd stop by."

"You wanted to establish your alibi," Linda said. "Don't be shocked, Cole. I know more than you'd have dreamed. My late husband was Leif Eriksson's brother. He was killed in an ambush setup for Leif. Matthew never had a chance, so Leif has done all that he could to make sure I'm taken care of."

Linda sat across from Cole in a pale lavender nightgown that did little to cover her nakedness. He felt himself becoming aroused. A lot of cleavage was showing and one leg was uncovered up to her thigh.

"I...ah...I best be going," Cole muttered.

"Nonsense," Linda said.

"I feel like I've intruded. I saw Doctor Garrett leaving."

Linda rose and crossed over to Cole. "He's my brother, silly. Now let's really establish that alibi," she said letting the gown fall off her shoulders.

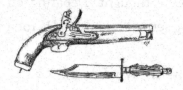

CHAPTER TWELVE

ANGUS, FLORENCE, AND SIDNEY RETURNED on Friday at midday. The man Eriksson was buying some tobacco and bought several cigars. When he and Cole were alone he handed him a small leather bag. It jingled when Cole took the bag.

"I appreciate you coming to our aid the other night. Joe thinks a lot of you."

Angus' wagon pulled up outside, before anything else could be said. Cole put the bag of coins away and followed Eriksson out the door.

Eriksson paused to light his cigar. A cloud of smoke engulfed the man's head. He waved his hand, clearing the little cloud of smoke. "Angus," Eriksson said. "Don't let anything happen to the man that rolls your cigars. They are worth the ride over."

His eyes took in the barrels in the back of the wagon, the red tax stamp apparent. Touching his hat, Eriksson whispered, "Smart." He then spoke to Florence, reaching out to lend a hand as she stepped off the wagon. "Good day to you, madam." He then walked over to his horse, mounted him and rode off.

"What did he want?" Angus asked.

Cole looked at his uncle. "He just rode up and asked for some Havana leaf cigars. He bought a twist of chewing tobacco and some pipe tobacco and then you came up."

"Did he ask for money?"

"No sir. But...ah...supplies did come in a couple of nights ago. I stored them as usual."

"By yourself?"

"No sir, I gave Jacob, the lad that helps Dalton, a meal and some small beer to help. He said that he'd rather have that than coin."

"I know the lad," Angus said. "He helps with the fishing boats when they come in and leave. They give him fresh fish and sometimes a coin. His father was a riding officer who was killed. I'm glad that you helped the boy."

Angus stepped close to Cole and whispered, "It's his mum that rolls the cigars. I keep the stuff around so that it looks like its done here, and I try my hand now and again. But it's the lad's mum, Agnes is her name, that does the rolling."

"A bloody good job she does too," Cole agreed. "I've been thinking of trying one."

"Aye, but have a care when ye start. They'll turn ye green," Angus said laughing.

***

SUNDAY WAS A BEAUTIFUL DAY. Cole arrived at Sir William's house at noon. Dinner was to be served at three o'clock so before he left the tavern Cole ate a thick slice of roast, some cheese, and bread. The meat and cheese were cold but good, and would tide him over until dinner was served.

A small carriage was arriving just as Cole drew up. The occupant was the widow, Kimberly Jordon. She was the owner of the Blue

Post Inn. Her husband had been a famous writer. Cole had dined with his aunt and uncle there on two occasions.

"One gets tired of one's own cooking," his Aunt Florence had said.

The meal had been outstanding and the wine was superb. No wonder Sir William held his meetings there when possible.

Once entering the house, the first person Cole saw was Mary, who was coming to meet Kimberly. He'd never seen her, only the portrait. As beautiful as the painting was, Mary was more so in real life.

Cole stood a step or two behind Kimberly and after they embraced Mary looked at Cole. Grasping her hands together a big smile fell over her face. "So you are the young man who has stolen my daughter's heart." Saying that, Anne's mother reached out her hand.

Cole, took the hand, bowed just so and kissed the back of Anne's mother's hand, remembering exactly as he was tutored. "If I may be so bold, Madam, I see where Anne gets her beauty." Pausing a beat, he added, "Sir William is a lucky man."

"Well said, young sir," Sir William had entered the room with Anne following.

Apparently both of them had heard his comments as Anne said, "I'll never be as pretty as mother." Cole knew better than to respond to that, so he just smiled.

Tea was served and polite conversation ensued. Mary talked about visiting her sick mother; Kimberly talked about adding an addition to her Blue Post Inn. The conversation finally drifted to Cole. He went over the part of awaiting word on his commission into the Dragoons. It was Kimberly who had asked if he was in Deal on vacation while waiting on his appointment.

"No, Madam, my father…and the Earl felt if I was going to be an officer then I should know something in regards to the men or type of men I will command."

"Quite so," Sir William agreed.

"It was felt in Canterbury that I would be offered preferential treatment no matter what I did. So I was sent off to my uncle's place to do a real day's work, although Phillip and I have had our days of cleaning the stable stalls." Everyone laughed at that. "Father wanted me to be around the everyday working man, to see how hard he works, what he has to do to raise his family, and the hardships that he faces."

"He wanted you to live it," Mary volunteered. "Your father is a smart man."

"Yes, Madam. Phillip is a midshipman on a frigate. By the time he becomes a lieutenant, he will have learned everything there is to know about the ship and the men who sail her. Whereas, to be a commissioned officer, all you need is an education, the right recommendations, and the funds to purchase your commission. There's nothing in the application that mentions one's experience handling people."

Sir William sat forward and grabbed his pipe. "I'd say that your father is a remarkable man, Cole. He must be, for the Earl to put him in such high regards. I think you'd do well to emulate him."

"Thank you, Sir William, I try."

A Negro in a mess coat entered, as if it was planned, "Dinner will be ready in fifteen minutes, Sir, should anyone care to freshen up."

The meal was one to remember, one that years down the road, Cole would look on with fondness. He was seated next to Anne, who continuously would rub her foot along his ankle and give him a great smile when he'd look at her. After the soup, a fish that was prepared in a delightful sauce was served first with a white wine to each person at the table. When the fish was finished, several servants came and cleaned the table including the utensils and wine glasses. A large beef roast was placed before Sir William, who carved several slices and then a servant took the platter around to each dinner guest. Vegetables were placed around the table and the beef was placed in the center after everyone had been served. A red wine was then poured. It was a tad sweet, Cole thought, but decided it was such for the women. Fruit tarts, pastries, and a pudding were served afterwards. Cole was now wishing that he'd left off the snack. It was around two hours when the dinner was complete.

Sir William took Cole in tow and showed him where to go to relieve himself. Anne's father then surprised Cole with the offer of a cigar.

"I've never really smoked," Cole admitted, "but so many people buy the Havana cigars from Uncle Angus that I've been tempted to try one."

"Some advice then, Cole, smoke no more than half of the cigar the first few times you smoke one." Sir William then leaned in and spoke as if man-to-man. "Also have a mint leaf handy if you've a notion for romance later. Most ladies don't like to kiss a man who's smoked a cigar. I don't chew but I'd think that would be more repulsive."

"Thank you for the advice, Sir. I shan't forget it."

One of Sir William's men played the piano. The women sang a few songs with the piano player. Cole was asked to join in but refrained.

"When I try to sing the dogs start barking," he japed.

When the evening was finally over, Anne held Cole back as Kimberly's rig was brought around. Sir William approached Cole, after they'd said good-bye to Kimberly.

"Anne's mother and I have decided to allow you to call on Anne here at the house. You will receive invitations and you may request visits. You are nearly a man, Cole, and I'll speak to you like one. I've seen the way my daughter turns heads when we walk or ride by a group of young men. I can only imagine how a man's blood will boil if he were to get close to her." Cole went to speak but Sir William held up his hand. "I know that you've kissed in the stable. It was written all over both of your faces."

Cole flushed but didn't try to deny it. Sir William continued, "Whether my daughter marries you or some other man, I want her to be pure...a virgin. So what I'm saying, sir...if ye blood boils, find you some woman to cool it. Hopefully, not some whore on Alfred Square or the wench that Angus employs."

"I shall take your words to heart, sir. I'll not disrespect Anne."

Sir William looked at Cole with a bit of a smile, "You better not or the next thing you'll take to heart is the end of my cavalry saber."

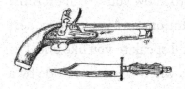

CHAPTER THIRTEEN

OLE WENT TO THE KITCHEN on Monday morning feeling like a new man. He'd gotten back so late that his aunt and uncle had already gone to bed. Angus was drinking coffee and waiting on his eggs and pork to be served when Cole entered the room.

He looked at his nephew with a smile. "I can see the visit to Sir William's went well."

"Aye, I'm allowed to call on Anne."

"Good, Cole, good." Angus had a change to his tone then; not an angry tone but not his usual either. "Joseph Lando came by yesterday. He has need of a driver to take a wagon to Canterbury. Two wagons really. He'll be driving one. He admitted that it's likely there's going to be a bit of contraband mixed in with the supplies, but since you'll be headed to Canterbury there will be no trouble. Were it anywhere but to see your mum and father, I'd say no. But he pointed out that I take the same route with the same risk. He also gave me his word if you were to be stopped he'll swear that you knew nothing about what you were hauling. You went along to see your parents and the Earl and maybe to check on your commission. He'll pay you as well," Angus threw in.

"I'll be glad to go, Uncle, if you won't need me."

"Lad, I must admit I've gotten used to you taking a lot of the load off your old uncle. But I know it's only temporary, so I best not get used to it."

"Then I'll go," Cole said.

***

Joe came around just before nine a.m. They rode horses to a warehouse behind the widow Linda Eriksson's house. The warehouse was situated in a stand of hardwood that was next to a low area that felt wet or soggy when you walked over it. You could take a horse from the widow's back property line to the warehouse but not a wagon.

Joe said to Cole, "The property is actually on John Stuart's land but you can't get to it from his property and it's not on the widow's land so there is room for denial from both of them. It will take an hour or more since the loaders are hand carrying the supplies. I will ride with you to see if Linda might be up to a guest. If so, you can stay while I go see Mary. If not, we'll both ride over to see Mary."

The widow was not home so, even though he felt in the way, Joe took Cole with him. He looked at Cole and said, "I'll not have you around them loading wagons. There's always the possibility that a Customs officer may come up. Once they are loaded you'll be in the clear."

The visit to the Stuarts was much different this trip. Mary was churning milk while her father was pressing already made butter into wooden butter molds using two wooden paddles that he called butter hands. He tasted some newly churned butter, at one point, saying that it needed more salt. Mr. Stuart, after adding more salt, started kneading the butter with his hand.

Joe looked over at Cole and said, "John's butter sells better than anybody's at the market, and next week is the start of market week in Deal."

Joe felt it was time to go after an hour of friendly chatter. They'd just got on the trail when the sound of a musket shot reached Joe. Riding on cautiously, the wagons were sighted and nothing seemed out of sorts.

"What was the gunshot for?" Joe asked.

"'E shot at a deer," a man said, pointing to another man. "Missed it 'e did."

Joe jumped off the horse, furious. "You fool. You draw attention to this area and these wagons by shooting at a deer. I ought to run you through. If we get caught, Dick, you better find a place to hide. A place far away from here because I'd not give two pence for your chances of living another day."

"Crazy bugger, 'e is," the first man who had spoken said, with the others agreeing. "I'll brain 'im meself if a duty man shows up, Mr. Lando."

"I might let you, Chester," Joe responded.

✸✸✸

JOE AND COLE HAD TRAVELED the five miles to Sandwich by noon, and had unloaded the supplies that were for Sandwich and were back on the road for Canterbury, which was eleven miles away. Joe had bought some bread and cheese for them to eat en route.

"Always eat when you can," Joe said. "You never know when you'll get the chance in my business."

They'd traveled about half the distance when Joe pulled his wagon and team off the road at a wide spot where a huge oak offered shade for the horses.

"I don't like to overtax the team," Joe said. "There's no need to ruin a good horse."

"Uncle Angus stopped and rested here as well," Cole offered. "I guess he is of the same mind." Joe nodded but didn't speak. Cole asked, after a few minutes, "Why doesn't Linda get married? She's a fine looking woman."

Joe pondered the question a moment or two. "I don't think she wants to take the chance of getting a husband involved with Leif Eriksson."

Cole replied, "Surely they could move."

"It would take a man of means to offer her the type of life she's used to."

"Joe!" Cole called to his friend. "Does she have a lot of...of suitors?"

"Not getting jealous, are you, lad?"

"No, but I don't want to be the cause of embarrassing anyone either."

"No, Cole, to my knowledge she doesn't. As far as I know, you are the only man that's shared her bed since her husband was killed."

"She told me the first night that she came was because of you."

Joe smiled, "I was a close friend with her husband so we have been close. I mentioned I wanted you to have a real woman and not some wench. I was thinking of her servant girl but she said she needed a discreet man in the worst way."

Cole smiled and then he thought of something. "You told me to say I'd been to the widow's house if the duty men stopped me."

"Aye, I did. There are always rumors, Cole. But like most rumors there's little or no basis to them. Her servant girl lives in one part of the house. Her name is Marge. I think she has a caller time and again. People just assume it's the widow they are seeing."

An idea came to Cole. "I bet it was Marge that Doctor Garrett was seeing, and not his sister."

The two men got their wagons underway and they arrived in Canterbury at four o'clock that afternoon. Cole saw the Earl's coach at Mifflin's as they arrived. He pointed it out to Joe.

"Go to him, lad. I'll come out to see you tomorrow."

Cole took his bag and went over to the coach. While waiting, he took out the pipes that he'd purchased for his father and the Earl. It was not long before both his father and the Earl came out of the Boar's Head Tavern. Both of the men were well dressed, so Cole was glad that he hadn't gone in search of the Earl and interrupted something.

The coachman was hurrying along behind them, trying to get to the coach before they did. Cole opened the door to the coach and placed the stepping stool down. The two men were so engrossed in their conversation that it was only when Cole said "Hello Father, my Lord," that the two men looked up smiling.

Cole's father embraced his son and then somewhat to Cole's surprise, so did the Earl. Riding back to Belcastle, Cole produced the two pipes.

"Thank you," the Earl said. "That was very kind of you, Cole." His father smiled and squeezed his hand.

"I have presents for mother and Catherine as well."

Cole's mother about smothered him with hugs and kisses and went on and on about the brush and comb he gave her. Catherine hugged him as well and hugged and kissed him even more when he gave her a set of tortoise shell combs to wear in her hair.

"You are a darling, brother," she proclaimed.

Cole, his mother and father, Catherine, and the Earl all dined together for dinner. Midway through the meal the Earl asked, "How is Sir William doing these days?"

"He was well when we last talked."

"I understand that he has a beautiful daughter."

"Yes, she is most charming, sir."

"I do believe Cole is blushing," Catherine teased.

To change the subject, Cole asked if there'd been any word on his commission.

"As a matter of fact there has," the Earl said. "There is some reorganization going on. It seems that we will be at war with France soon, and we've not recovered from the war with the Colonies. The general tells me that he thinks you'd be of little use until the reorganization is completed. He expects that to take most of a year the way Parliament moves. But have no fear, Cole, he has assured me you will be one of the first that he calls."

The talk then turned to Deal and how Angus was keeping him occupied. Cole's mother beamed when he told them that he'd been trusted enough to run the tavern while his aunt and uncle went to London.

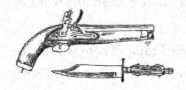

CHAPTER FOURTEEN

OLE WAS LYING IN HIS bed, his mind drifting from Anne to the widow Linda. They'd returned to Deal a week ago, today. He'd been to visit Anne twice and that night he'd gone to see Linda. She'd said that her monthly curse was upon her so Cole had stayed for awhile, just long enough to be polite and enjoy refreshments with her. He'd have stayed longer but she seemed very preoccupied, so after an hour he'd departed.

He could hear voices outside his window. *A ship must be expected tonight*, he thought. Cole realized sleep would not come, after a while, so he dressed and went out. He headed down to Beach Street and to the shore.

The tide was coming in and gentle waves washed up on the beach. He could hear voices up ahead, undoubtedly the last of the tubmen making for their rendezvous. Bored, Cole ventured forth. He wanted to see how the boats landed ashore and the tubmen taking their loads.

He was almost on them, in the dark, before he realized it. An old fishing boat lay discarded on the beach. Ducking down behind it, he watched as one, and then two and three boats landed on the beach. He marveled at how quickly a tubman put a barrel over his back and across his shoulder. He'd been watching the tubmen gather their loads when a movement caught his eye. At first, he thought it was more tubmen coming, but suddenly he realized that they were not tubmen at all. These men were armed with muskets. They were duty men.

Cole knelt down even further and even slid down toward the stern of the boat. What should he do? If he shouted out, he'd surely be caught and maybe even shot. *Was Joe out there*, he wondered. Not likely, if he was though, he'd be at the top of the road. Surely, there would be duty men closing in from there as well. He had to think of something to warn the tubmen and Joe, if indeed, he was there.

The stern of the deserted fishing boat had a hole in it and appeared to be rotten. A thought came to Cole, if he could tear off a bit and toss it, maybe that would be enough to alert the smugglers that they were about to be attacked. While he tugged on a plank, something told him that this was wrong. The smugglers were breaking the law. One day, in fact, he may be part of the army that rose up against the smugglers. Damn it, though, Joe might be up there and he was his friend.

A board broke loose and Cole grabbed the end and flung it for all he was worth. The surf was coming in and the board hit the wet sand flat sided, making a loud 'splat'. Two of the batmen whirled around looking down the beach.

Somebody caught sight of the duty man and yelled, "Duty men."

It was followed by a musket firing, and then another. The air was rent with the sound of gunfire. Cole, still kneeling down behind the boat, could see orange flames leap out from the muskets as they were fired into the darkness. He heard a sickening thud at one point, and a man cried out in pain. There were men running, shouting and some cursing. One man jumped on the bow of a boat that he had pushed back into the dark waters. The tide was now almost full and Cole's clothes were soaked as he tried to make himself smaller at the stern of the rotten boat. He feared that the tide would move it at any moment.

One of the duty men, at one point, paused beside the bow of the boat, lifted his weapon and fired. He then reloaded and ran on. The gunfire, shouts, and curses soon ended. Cole waited a good half hour before he ran back down the beach toward Deal. He took off his wet clothes and hung them over the top rails of the stalls in the stable. He'd just started back into the house when Sidney opened the back door.

"You startled me," Cole swore.

"Where have you been?"

"I went down to the beach and got tripped up and fell into the water."

"I bet," Sidney snorted. "You went to meet some wench."

Cole started to deny it but thought, *'let him think that'*. It's better than explaining what did happen. "You keep yer mouth closed," Cole hissed.

"No worries, I know about those things. You are just lucky that you got back safe. The guards are out tonight."

"Guards?" Cole inquired.

"Yes, the preventive services people."

"I wonder if they fired their guns," Cole said. We...er I thought I heard a shot."

"We'll know tomorrow," Sidney offered.

❖❖❖

THE FOLLOWING DAY AND FOR days afterward, the talk was all about the raid on the smugglers. The one smuggler who'd been killed was placed in a gibbet along the main road. His decaying body was being torn apart by crows and acted as a grim reminder of the law against smuggling. Joe had dropped by and Cole was elated to see that his friend had not been caught by the duty men.

When they were alone, Joe whispered, "It wasn't even our group. Some small time actor who didn't know how to keep his mouth shut."

"Joe, I was there. I alerted the smugglers before the duty men got in place good."

"You young fool," Joe hissed.

"I was worried that you'd get caught, Joe."

Joe took a deep breath and listened to Cole's story. He softened realizing that Cole had risked his neck, thinking he was saving his friend. "You'll know from now on," Joe promised. "But don't ever risk your neck for the likes of me, Cole."

"You're my friend, Joe."

"Aye, I am and its time that we get busy teaching you to fight."

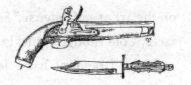

CHAPTER FIFTEEN

MARKET WEEK STARTED THE FRIDAY after the last trial of those caught smuggling. The smuggler was sentenced to prison and would be escorted to London by a detail of the King's preventive service men. The air of the town changed with the trial over, and market week starting.

People talked freely, waved at passersby, and business at the tavern imprsoved. The market drew buyers and sellers, not only from Deal, but from nearby farms and villages from the surrounding countryside. Some of the wealthier or more prominent farmers paid a fee to set up official booths, while others set up stands outside the market grounds. The baker and butcher set up booths and had large displays of their products.

Angus paid a fee and set up a wagon to sell ale and small beer. Sir William's coach drew up and Sir William stepped down, helping his wife and daughter to exit also. Cole ran up to greet them.

Anne saw him first and a big smile creased her face. It immediately turned into a frown and she exclaimed, "Cole, what happened to your face?" Sir William and Mary looked closer at Cole.

Cole touched his face and said, "I have been taking instructions on the art of self defense." Seeing a frown gather on Anne's parents' faces, Cole thought quickly. "The general commanding the Prince of Wales Dragoons has told the Earl that we will be at war with France very soon. It was recommended that I be able to defend myself beyond the ways of a gentleman. That as an officer leading his men in combat, I have to be able to fight...hand to hand combat if such a situation develops."

Sir William nodded his agreement adding, "It seems that our island nation will eternally find itself set upon by those who would inflict their will upon us. It does my heart good to see such young men as you rise to defend our country, Cole. It saddens me though that we must always risk the lives of so many brave lads."

Cole swallowed hard. Sir William had unknowingly created a bit of fear in Cole. Prior to Sir William's comments, his biggest fear was that Sir William would ask who made the recommendation that he learn to fight. Anne took Cole's arm and her mother laid a hand across his shoulder. The hammer fell then.

"Who is your instructor, Cole? One of the officers at Deal castle."

Damn, here it comes, thought Cole. "No, sir. Joseph Lando, Sir William. I hear that he is the best."

Sir William paused in his stride. After a moment, he started walking again. "For the type of training you need to undergo, I can think of no better. He has a reputation as a pugilist of some renown. I'm not fond of his benefactor, though. Sir George Aylward is rumored to be the money man behind the biggest smuggling operation in all of Kent. Rumor, mind you. There's never been any proof."

"Do you think that he was behind this recent operation, William?" Anne's mother asked.

"No, Mary that was a small time operator. We got wind of this a week before the boats landed."

Anne's hand found Cole's as they walked through the market, and they walked hand in hand. Cole had never really gone to the market in Canterbury, so he was impressed with his first experience.

Farmers brought not only produce to sell, but also livestock... horses, cows, one fine looking bull, pigs, goats and even a few sheep. Cole spied the Stuarts' booth. They had brought the butter that Cole saw them making, but also eggs, cheese, and even a few crates with chickens. John and Mary both gave Cole warm greetings. When they came to a booth selling flowers, Cole bought a bundle for Anne and her mother.

Mary paused, near the end of the first aisle, "I fear that we are near the fishermen's stalls."

The odor of fish was definitely in the air, and more so when a man walked past with a sack of oysters over his shoulder. They cut between two booths and started up the next aisle. This aisle had more things a woman would buy.

"I didn't know they sold these types of items at the market," Cole said.

"Yes, the women sell their wares and take the profit and buy cookware, buckets, cloth to make clothes, some shoes and such. Many people send their servants to purchase meats, vegetables, and fruits, and even use the opportunity to buy something special for their girls." Anne and Cole looked at each other and smiled.

When they were leaving, they saw a group of people who were standing around a man who'd set up a table, and was running a shell game.

Sir William shook his head. "There are also the gamblers, pick pockets, and beggars."

Cole paused at a stand selling bright ribbons with crosses. He purchased one for Anne, after asking permission.

"It feels so smooth, like silk," Anne said.

"It's probably from France," her mother said, feeling of it.

"Without the taxes having been paid also," her father added. "Otherwise, it would not be so cheap."

The driver spoke when they got back to the family coach, "Looks like they're putting up a boxing ring, sir."

"I'm not surprised. Aylward likes to put up his champ every so often." Sir William looked at Cole, "You may get a chance to see your instructor practice his art."

"Yes sir," Cole said. He knew that a guinea was being offered to anyone who could beat Joe in the three rounds; his Uncle Angus had told him.

***

THE SUN WAS GOING DOWN when Cole was able to get away from the beer and ale wagon. Business had essentially come to a halt as people made their way to the fight ring. Three men, so far, had signed up to fight Joe. Four had actually signed up, but one was so drunk that he couldn't stand. The rules were standard. The bouts would last until someone was knocked down. Each fighter then would go to his corner. A new round would start after one minute. This was a bare knuckle fight.

The first fighter came in. He was a slim, muscled man who made his living fishing. He'd fought several of the rogues on Alfred Square but it was soon evident that he was no match for Joe. The man weaved in and feinted swiftly, and threw one hand right. It never touched Joe, yet he felt a smashing fist in his side and then an upper cut to his chin as Joe put together two hard punches. The fisherman went down and didn't toe the line for the next round. The fight was over.

The next man was a farmer's son. He was big, moved slowly but from the size of his arms if he hit you, the fight would probably be over. He outweighed Joe by at least one hundred pounds. The bell rang and Joe went to the center of the ring to shake hands like he'd done the previous fight. Only the farm boy knocked Joe's hand aside with his left and threw a looping right. It would have knocked Joe's head off had he not been quick; but Joe was quick. His head darted back, and the huge fist just grazed his chin and glanced across Joe's chest and shoulder. A big boo...went up with jeers at the unsportsmanlike punch by the farm boy. Joe took a step or two back. He started circling the farm boy and jabbing with his left. Jab...jab...jab. Joe kept jabbing, not at the face, but at the big boy's ribs with a couple of jabs hitting him in the gut. The farm boy awkwardly turned as Joe circled him. He once threw such a hard punch, it threw him off balance, causing him to fall into the ropes. Joe could have ended it there but he stepped back and waited until the boy righted himself. This caused the crowd to cheer and shout good-natured japes. Joe then went to work.

He circled the farm boy faster now. Jabs to the face, jabs to the chest, and jabs to the ribs. Joe then reversed his movement and Cole almost didn't see it. He reversed the way he circled, slammed a left into the farm boy's gut and then as the boy bent over, he hit him on the chin with a right so hard that Cole was sure he heard the boy's jaw break. Down the boy went.

Down,..and he didn't get back up. The fight was over for him. The fight seemed like it had taken forever but Cole heard someone say four minutes. Someone threw a bucket of water on the farm boy and then four men picked him up and carried him from the ring.

Cole thought the big oaf deserved what he got after treating Joe so, but he also couldn't help but feel sorry for him.

The third fighter was a man built much like Joe. He was a bit above average height, had broad shoulders, and unlike the muscle bound farm boy, his muscles were well formed and toned but not bulging. He even had a muscled abdomen. Cole thought to himself, *you'd break your hand hitting that 'un in the gut. Joe's got his work cut out for him.*

"That ain't no bairn," Uncle Angus said.

The crowd gathered closer, looking at Joe's next opponent. Bets were being made by several. Leif Eriksson was in the middle of those making bets. Once both fighters were in the ring, the bets stopped. Listening to the men around him, Cole realized that the man Joe was fighting was an army sergeant. In his corner, he was able to see an officer–a captain, another sergeant and a few soldiers.

When the bell rang, the two men toed the line and they both reached out to shake. The rules had been explained and both men went to their corners. It was easy to see that the sergeant knew what he was doing as the fight started. He was fast, maybe faster than Joe. He was also a puncher. His flat nose was evidence that he'd been in some fights, so there was little doubt he knew the game. The sergeant came in fast. He smashed into Joe's midsection. As he did, Joe hooked a left to the sergeant's head. It made him pause and blink. His ear began to swell.

Joe got reckless then and took one on the chin that knocked him down. Joe sat there looking at the sergeant, maybe with a bit of respect. One man said that's a first and another said it wasn't. When the bell rang again, Joe met the sergeant at the center of the ring with a suddenness that startled the sergeant. Joe stabbed a left to the sergeant's mouth that had blood flowing, and then blasting a fist to the chest, followed by one to the side of the head again, he put the sergeant down. From the time the bell had rung, Joe had floored the sergeant in a matter of seconds. The crowd roared. Both men were glistening with sweat. Joe wiped his face in his corner. They poured water over the sergeant to wash away the blood but a trickle still ran down the side of his head from the split ear.

When the bell rang both men stepped to the center and started slugging it out. Joe's eyes seemed to blaze with fury. The two men began to slug it out toe to toe, both of them determined to win. Joe punched with a fury as the rage of battle spun him on. Then a trip, not a knockdown but a trip, had Joe down, so the round was officially over. They'd get another round. When the bell rang, both men charged out, coming together in a crash of blows. The sergeant stabbed a wicked left to Joe's head that split the eyebrow. The blood flowing into Joe's eye made it hard for him to see. A groan went through the crowd. The sergeant moved in, sensing a victory, but Joe caught him with a right that jolted him. He fell back stumbling. Another roar came from the crowd. Joe paused, allowing the man to come off the rope. When he was away from the ropes, Joe threw a chopping blow that split the sergeant's eye. Joe was almost like a crazed animal now. He hooked the sergeant under the chin and then slammed his right into the sergeant's chest right over the heart. It was the hardest punch that many had ever seen. The sergeant stopped dead in his tracks and fell backwards. The fight was over. Joe Lando, battered and bloody, had won again.

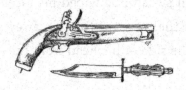

CHAPTER SIXTEEN

JOE CLIMBED OUT OF THE ring with a towel pressed against his eyebrow. Mary was there and in his arms crying and kissing him all over. Joe saw Cole and put an arm across his shoulder. Someone offered Joe a beer, which he took a swallow of and then poured the rest over his head. A wagon was brought around and Joe got in along with Mary, her father, Sir George Aylward, and Doctor Garrett. They drove over to the doctor's office for Joe to get stitched up.

Angus walked up beside Cole. "That was a fight, lad. No mistake about it."

As Cole walked with his uncle, they passed Leif Eriksson. The man should have been happy. There was little doubt that he'd won money on Joe. He did not look happy though. He looked angry, in fact.

***

THE LIGHTS TO LINDA'S HOUSE came into view as Cole rounded the bend. Seeing the lights eased his mind. Cole had a sensation that someone was following him since turning off the main road. Once he was sure that he had heard a horse neigh. He turned in the saddle but didn't see anything. A sound like a stick cracking another time made him turn again. He wondered if a highwayman might be out. He'd passed a few travelers walking or in wagons going home from the market.

Earlier, Cole had been walking with his uncle toward the beer wagon when he felt a tug on his sleeve. A cute young lady said, "Please sir," handing him a note and giving a small curtsey. When he took the note, she turned and ran off.

Angus smiled, "An admirer."

"No, Uncle," Cole said and then realized the girl was Linda's servant girl, Marge. He smiled back at his uncle, "An admirer's messenger."

Cole put the note in his pocket until they had gotten the wagon and taken it back to the tavern. He read the note once he was in his room. It simply said, "We might have tea and dessert if you were to stop by tonight around eight." Cole had helped with the chores and then took a bath.

Sidney came in while Cole was dressing, "Going to see your lady friend." Cole winked and smiled, but didn't say anything. Sidney smiled then, "Don't go down to the beach again, you'll ruin your shoes." They both laughed at that.

When Cole rode up to the house, he spotted Doctor Garrett's wagon. *Maybe Linda really meant tea and dessert,* he thought, feeling disappointed. A black man came from the back of the house to take Cole's horse. He hadn't been there before but he seemed to know his way around.

The door opened while he was still watching the man. "That's Saul," Linda said. "He's my stable man."

Cole nodded, "I've not seen him before."

"I sent him to Dover," Linda said not saying for what.

Cole quickly asked about Doctor Garrett. "He's visiting with Marge," Linda said.

"I wanted to warn him," Cole said. "I felt like I was being followed or watched while riding here. I wonder if some rogue might be about."

Linda paused a moment and then stepped into the kitchen and out the back door calling for Saul. When she stepped back in, she said, "I told Saul and he'll accompany Gary home."

"Gary?" Cole asked.

"My brother, Gary Garrett," Linda replied.

Cole shook his head. He took in the sway of Linda's body as the two of them walked from the kitchen. She had to be the most sensuous woman he'd ever seen.

Linda sat down in a chair and picked up a glass that was on a side table. She handed the glass to Cole saying, "Pour us a brandy, Cole." As he did so, Linda said, "I saw you with Sir William's daughter today. I thought that you two looked sweet walking so."

Damme, Cole thought. *Is she going to be angry or jealous that I was with Anne?* He filled both glasses. His face must have betrayed his thoughts as he turned to hand Linda her glass.

"Don't worry, darling," Linda said. "I'm not a jealous old widow. I really mean it. You two looked sweet together. It brought back memories of when I first met Matthew." She looked distant for a moment. "No, Cole, I'm not jealous, envious maybe."

She took a swallow of her brandy. "What we have, my love is very special; something that I've needed. I know that it will not last and may even come to an abrupt halt."

Cole thought Linda was talking about his leaving at first, but then he realized it was more...much more but he didn't push her. In fact, his mind was suddenly on another thought.

When Linda had reached for her brandy, her nightgown had opened up a little bit. Half of her left breast was uncovered and had drawn his attention to it.

Linda noticed his gaze. "Like what you see?" she asked.

"Most assuredly...as much as I can see."

"Would you like to see more?" Cole stepped toward Linda. "Blow out the lamp," she whispered.

Cole did so, never letting his gaze stray for more than a moment. Flames in the fireplace caused flickering shadows to dance on the walls. He walked over and knelt in front of Linda. He untied the nightgown pulling it open. Her skin looked like cream in the faint light. He ran his hands over her breasts. He raised up and kissed her lips long and hard, and then kissed her neck. She leaned forward giving Cole greater access and enjoying the feel of his lips, his warm breath on her sensitive skin. She began to moan and when his mouth found her nipple she grasped his head, crushing it against her breast.

"God, Cole," she whispered.

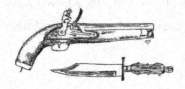

CHAPTER SEVENTEEN

OLE WOKE THE FOLLOWING MORNING when the sun was just climbing over the horizon. The wind was blowing just enough to make the limbs of a large ash tree sway. He'd gotten home as the long case clock in his aunt and uncle's quarters struck four a.m. He and Linda had made love until both were spent from their passion, then cuddled tightly in her large bed. Cole had woken up feeling the call of nature. His bladder was about to bust. He eased out of the house not wanting to use the chamber pot for fear of waking Linda. Hopefully, at that early hour, someone would not come by and see a naked man pissing off her porch. He tiptoed back into Linda's bedroom. She lay curled up, with her head barely on the edge of the pillow. The one that he'd shared with her. A sheet only partially covered her nakedness.

My, she is radiant, he thought. It would be easy to love this woman. He did love her, in fact, but it was a love that could never be made public. He was eighteen. A man, most anyone would agree, but she was thirty-six; twice his age. He was still young and he could only hope his wife would be as passionate as she was when she reached thirty-six.

Linda had no children. She had lost one in childbirth and the other only weeks after being born. Her husband then died in an ambush by duty men. He shouldn't have even been there, but he'd gone to deliver a message for his brother. Cole felt his heart going out to this woman who had lost everything...her husband and her children. It was no wonder that she was lonely. Some may call it wrong what they did, but Cole Buckley was determined that he'd do his best to show her his love and loyalty.

He had dressed as quickly and quietly as he could. He did not want someone seeing him leave and adding to the rumors that abounded. He found a writing quill and paper on her little desk. He wrote, 'I cherish our time together.' He placed the paper on the pillow and left.

Back at the tavern, he'd gotten off his horse and, with his hand over its nose to keep it from nickering, had walked the horse from the street and put it in the stable. He'd sat on the bed removing his boots when the clock chimed four a.m. He quickly undressed and fell to sleep...a contented sleep.

Something woke him. Was it the wind? He heard, in the distance, a long low rumble of thunder that grew louder as it came closer. He heard Sidney's door open, so he was up as well. He went to his door and softly called, "Sidney."

The boy turned and walked to Cole. "I think we are in for a blow. I'm going to get some wood and fill the fire box before it gets wet."

"I'll help," Cole volunteered. He slipped into his britches and boots and grabbed a shirt. Outside the wind was increasing.

"It was like this when I lost me mum and father," Sidney said.

Cole immediately felt sorry for the boy. *Phillip*, he thought suddenly. *Is Phillip at sea in this weather or is he in port somewhere?* A small prayer came to him and he repeated the parts that he could remember as Sidney loaded up his arms with stove wood. He'd just returned for a second load when lightning struck nearby.

The ground shook and Cole could feel his hair on his arms stand up. Sidney worked faster, his face pale in the dim light. Cole returned for one more load and as Sidney stacked wood on his outstretched arms he realized that the sky had darkened as clouds rolled in. Leaves were falling from the trees and floated on the air before hitting the ground and scattering about.

"Maybe we should put the horses in their stalls," Cole said as the wind banged the stable door open and closed. Had he forgotten to latch it when he'd rode in during the wee hours. He went over to push the door to, but something blocked it.

He saw, looking down, a foot...a small foot, a girl's foot. "Sidney," he yelled against the wind, "go get a lantern and tell Uncle Angus to come quickly."

"He may be asleep."

"Then wake him up. Dammit, Sidney, go."

Uncle Angus was undoubtedly awake, probably awakened by them toting wood inside. He came out carrying the lantern and Cole motioned him over to the stable. They opened the stable door and there on the ground lay Peg. Her clothes had been ripped from her body and she'd been shot in the chest. Her face was bruised. Blood drained from her nose and someone had busted her mouth.

"Lord, Peg, look what you've done and got yourself into. Oh... she's alive," Cole said.

"Aye, lad, but I fear not for long. Off with you, Cole, run get Doctor Garrett. Sidney, go tell Florence to put on some hot water and bring a blanket. I'll not have her lying there naked. When you've done that, lad, go fetch the constable. Off with you now, lad."

Cole ran the few blocks to Doctor Garrett's. As he ran, he wondered if it had been the gunshot that had awakened him. Something had and he didn't think it had been the weather. Cole mounted the steps at the doctor's house two at a time. He banged on the door so loudly that his knuckles hurt. Garrett came to the door with a candle lit.

"Alright, I'm coming for Christ's sake." He opened the door and saw Cole and took a step back.

"Hurry Doctor Garrett, Peg's been shot in the chest."

The doctor, instantly wide awake, turned back toward his bedroom. He put his britches on over his bed clothes, pulling his suspenders in place. He slipped his shoes on with his stockings. He grabbed his bag and a bottle of something from his medicine cabinet.

A fine sprinkle had started to fall as they went out the door. Walking at a fast pace, they made it back to the stable in no time.

The doctor said, while examining Peg, "Is there a board or something to act as a stretcher and carry her inside the tavern?"

Sidney got the board that they had laid across two barrels to make a bar of sorts at the market. Rolling Peg slightly, they got the board under her. With Angus and Cole toting the board, Sidney ran and opened the doors, holding them open until they were in the taproom.

"Light some lanterns," the doctor ordered.

Cole and Sidney went to work getting light into the taproom. Taking the bottle of medicine out of his bag, Doctor Garrett had Angus open Peg's mouth. He drew up a dropper full of the medicine. He counted thirty drops and then stopped. He then took a clean kitchen rag and dipped it in the pan of water that Florence had brought over. He cleaned the wound and asked Angus for his best gin. He poured this over the wound and then over his surgical instruments which lay in a pan.

"It's said the alcohol helps with the ill humours that attack such wounds." Once the blood was cleared away, Garrett said, "There's no powder burns on the skin. That's good. Had the weapon been pressed against the body the ball would likely have entered the chest cavity. Were that so, Peg would have no chance."

He pushed on Peg's chest and then put a shiny probe in the wound and followed its path. "The ball has hit the breast bone and traveled along the ribs until the ball lies under her left breast. She tried to turn away from the shooter undoubtedly."

After a few minutes, the doctor took out a pair of forceps used to remove bullets. He pushed and tugged and finally came out with an odd shaped ball.

The doctor asked, "Was she nude when you found her?"

Cole answered, "Yes, I did see her clothes on the dirt though."

"Was there a hole in them?"

"No, I don't think so," Cole replied.

"Good," Doctor Garrett said. "I won't have to worry about debris in the wound."

Cole was not sure he understood what the good doctor meant but he nodded. After putting a large dressing on Peg, the doctor wrapped it in place with Cole holding the girl up. The doctor cleaned Peg's face, after finishing the dressing, and then looked at her hands. Blood was on her fingers and while examining her one hand and fingers, he immediately picked up the other hand.

He said, after a moment, "If her assailant is still around, he should be identified easily enough. It appears that Peg has clawed her attacker pretty good. She has flesh and blood under her nails. Look for a man with a clawed face and you will probably have your man. He will tote Peg's marks a lifetime I would imagine."

A knock on the door rang out. "Probably the constable," Angus volunteered.

"Let's get a gown over the girl before anyone else comes in," Garrett recommended. "She will be out for a while, but is there a place close by where we can keep her?"

"We have an extra room," Aunt Florence said. "She'll have us to care for her here."

It was then that Cole realized it had never occurred to him to find out where Peg lived.

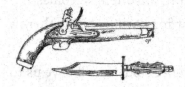

CHAPTER EIGHTEEN

COLE WAS AMAZED AT HOW quickly the word got out. People were stopping by the tavern on Sunday morning checking on Peg. Cole had been invited to Sir William's house for Sunday dinner. He caught sight of Kimberly Jordan's carriage as he rode and realized that this must be a Sunday ritual, her visiting with Anne's mother. Cole rode up beside Kimberly. She smiled and they rode the rest of the way alongside one another.

The dinner followed the same pattern as his last visit only a rack of lamb was offered first in place of the fish. Once they delved into the main course, the subject of Peg being shot came up. Cole gave a good narrative of the situation including the distinct possibility that it was the gunshot that woke him up. He said nothing of his not getting in until four a.m. He did say Doctor Garrett had made it plain that the man who shot Peg was sure to have extensive claw marks on his face, which would surely serve as a means of identifying the attacker.

"Why would the girl be out at such an ungodly hour?" Mary, Anne's mother asked.

"We have all wondered that, especially in the stables," Cole admitted.

"Maybe someone wanted to murder the poor girl, and wanted her where she was sure to be found," Kimberly volunteered.

"A bad business regardless," Sir William said as he asked a servant for a slice of pie.

The dinner soon broke up and Cole followed Sir William as he had previously to where they could relieve themselves and freshen up.

While Cole was drying his hands, Sir William spoke. His words shocked Cole, but as he was drying his face, he hoped that it didn't show. It also gave him time to think.

"Aye, sir, if you are referring to what I think you are. I took your advice, sir, and found a way to relieve pent up humours. The lady in question is not a prostitute nor is there any misgiving in regards to romance."

Sir William looked at Cole. "I have heard rumors."

"As have I," Cole answered. "Frankly, I asked the lady were there any other gentlemen callers who might take exception to our visits. She swore there was not but did admit to the rumors." He then asked a question. "Was it your man who was trying to discreetly follow me? I must say he failed miserably."

Sir William replied, "Not my man exactly. He was a riding officer. There has been word that the smugglers often store goods in that direction."

This was information that Cole was sure that Joe should know. He then thought Joe probably already knew this. "Sir William, if I may, sir. If the riding officer can't be more discreet than he was trailing me, he'll never catch one of the rogues in the free trade."

Sir William looked at Cole, "Where did you hear that term, 'free trade'?"

Cole looked at the man that may be his future father-in-law. "Where have I not heard it, Sir William?" He glanced over as he and Sir William entered a room.

Anne was chewing on her lips. Cole suddenly thought and said, "If you recall, sir, at the booth where I bought Anne's ribbon and cross, you said for such a price it had to be part of the free trade."

"Have you heard it in Angus' tavern?"

Cole stopped once more, "As I said, sir, there's rarely been a street or shop or inn that I've not heard the word or innuendo, including this house."

"God's truth," Mary said. "William stop being the magistrate long enough to be your daughter's father. You will not treat Cole or any other guest as if he's on trial in your court. Why don't you ask your wife who shops in Deal how many times and where she has heard the term? I shall tell you plainly, William...everywhere and everyday I'm in town. It should not surprise you, if you'd admit it, the tea we drink, the tobacco you smoke and more than a few of the clothes we wear came from cloth brought in by the free trade."

Cole swallowed hard and was sure he'd never seen a man accosted so by a woman, wife or no. Sir William was speechless and pale. Anne had sidled up to Cole and, taking his hand, they made their way out the entrance behind her father. The two walked around the house, and when Anne was sure they were behind some hedges high enough that they couldn't be seen she stopped. She put her arms around Cole's neck and pulled his head down to kiss him. The kiss was long and passionate. When they broke apart, she smiled and kissed him again. This time she put her tongue in his mouth. After a moment, the kiss ended.

"Did you like that?" Anne asked.

"Yes...yes," Cole stammered.

Anne pulled a penny novel from somewhere in the folds of her dress. It was a very graphic novel with drawings of couples engaging in very erotic acts and positions.

"Where did you get that?" Cole asked.

"Dalton's sister, Belinda, gave it to me. Her father and some of the servant girls read them and they try to have sex like the people in the pictures."

"Was that in there? Putting your tongue in my mouth," Cole asked.

Anne nodded. "You liked it. I know you did."

Cole couldn't deny that he liked it.

"There's more but we'll save it until after we are married. It takes my breath thinking about it," Anne said in a coarse whisper.

"Mine too," Cole admitted.

"I know," Anne said. "I felt you against me. We must never do that again, because it's not fair to raise your humours without being able to relieve them." She laughed a mischievous laugh. "Besides anyone looking at you would know that we'd been doing something," she said this looking down at Cole's pants. Seeing where her gaze was, Cole turned red from embarrassment. "Don't worry, it's not visible now."

"When..." Cole breathed easier. Taking her hand, he whispered, "You should get rid of that book. If your mother found it, it would be bad. Worse, if your father found it."

Anne just laughed without committing to doing away with the book.

They finished walking around the house and then sat on the porch. Before long, Kimberly's carriage was brought around. Kimberly, along with Anne's parents, came out within a minute or so.

"I need to be going as well, I guess," Cole said.

As they said good-bye to Kimberly, Cole asked the groomsman to bring his horse. The horse was soon brought around and Cole said his good-bye. When he took the first step down, he felt Anne tug at his arm. As he turned around, Anne gave him a quick kiss on the lips...right in front of her parents.

She smiled quickly and said, "That will keep you thinking of me until we see each other again."

Cole smiled. It was her way of making him think of the other kiss.

"Ah...just a minute," Sir William called to Cole.

Damme, the little wench, Cole thought.

Sir William walked up to Cole and placed a hand on his shoulder in a friendly gesture, removing his pipe from his mouth with his other hand. Looking over Sir William's shoulder, Cole could see Mary holding Anne's hand looking at her husband.

"I want to apologize for being so intrusive in my questions. I've no doubt you've heard the term every day since you've been here, as my wife pointed out."

"There's no need to apologize," Cole said trying to salve the verbal lashes Mary had inflicted. "I know that you have your daughter's best interest in mind when asking such questions."

Sir William smiled and Cole had the feeling that he'd just managed to make his relationship with Anne's father stronger and more certain.

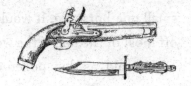

CHAPTER NINETEEN

I
T WAS MID-AFTERNOON ON MONDAY when Joe walked into the
tavern. His eye was still swollen some and he had yellowish
bruises on his face. He asked how Peg was and asked if he could see
her. Angus thought a moment or two and then motioned for Joe
to follow him.

The doctor had been there that morning and was concerned
about Peg. She was running a fever and her wounds looked red and
inflamed. Joe placed his hand on Peg's forehead as he bent down
and whispered to her. She opened her eyes for a moment, gave a
smile and squeezed Joe's hand. He stayed with Peg for a moment
more and then walked back to the taproom.

"Angus, I've a need to borrow Cole for a few days if you both
agree. I need to make a trip to London, and to be honest I don't feel
up to taking the trip alone. I'll pay Cole and to set you at ease, we'll
not be hauling any goods."

Angus looked at Cole and then at Joe. "It's been slow since Peg
was shot, so now is a good time if Cole is of a mind to travel."

Cole was quick to respond. "Sure, I won't be seeing Anne until
Saturday."

Joe smiled, "That will work then."

Cole put clothes in a bag and went out front where Joe had a small one-horse rig. It would seat two with a top that would keep off most of the rain if the weather turned bad.

Joe said, as they pulled off, that they would make a couple of short stops. The first one would be at Linda's, and if she was agreeable Cole could spend time with her while he went to the Stuart farm to see Mary and her father. He wouldn't be long, an hour or so.

Cole saw Saul looking to see who was coming down the lane. Marge was hanging clothes on a line and Linda was walking back from the chicken coop with a basket of eggs. She walked up to the rig and greeted Joe and Cole.

"Would you care for some tea?" Linda asked.

Joe nodded to his friend, "Cole might. I have to go see John Stuart for an hour or so."

Linda smiled and said, "And Mary, I'd wager."

"You'd win," Joe said.

Linda looked at Cole, "You are welcome to stay, of course. I still have a few chores."

Cole was climbing out of the rig. "I'd be glad to help," he offered.

"It's settled then." Joe spoke again, only this time his tone was firm. Almost like there was steel in his voice, a manner which Cole had only heard him speak but once, and that was when the custom agents had raided the smugglers. He'd called Cole a fool, and then softened his voice.

He did not soften his voice this time, "Have you seen Leif?" he asked.

"No...not in several days," she said. "Not since the market. Why, Joe... why do you ask?"

"Personal," he replied. "If you see him, tell him that I want to see him." He turned the rig around and headed back down the lane.

Cole took the egg basket from Linda, letting his hand linger on hers. "I meant it when I said that I'd help you with the chores, Linda. I'd never barge in on you expecting…"

"Favors," Linda provided the word.

Cole smiled, "Yes." Now Linda smiled.

They took the eggs over to the well and poured water in a pan. They washed the eggs then and Cole dried them.

When the eggs were clean and dried, Linda shouted to Marge, "Cole and I are going inside for tea." She put a pot of water on to heat up for the tea when she was inside the kitchen.

"Linda," Cole called to his special friend, "can I ask you a private question between us?"

Linda smiled, "Of course."

"Have you stuck your tongue in a man's mouth when you kissed him?"

Linda looked at Cole. She set the can of tea down and came to him. She put her hand behind Cole's head and gave him a long passionate kiss like Anne had done but more heated. When she finished with the kiss, her hand drifted down to his crotch and felt his stiffness.

"I do that when I want this to react like it has," she said. It took Cole a moment to catch his breath.

"Some are calling that a French kiss, though I know of no reason why," she said. "People have been doing it for centuries."

"I see," Cole stammered.

Linda looked at Cole a minute. "Did your little girlfriend do that to you?"

"She did," Cole admitted. "Her girlfriend gave her a penny novel from Covent Garden. It was very graphic and risqué."

Linda smiled, "I can imagine. Did you like what you saw?"

"It did stir me," Cole admitted.

Linda smiled again, "You stir me, Cole Buckley, in ways I'd never thought possible."

***

WHEN JOE RETURNED, COLE SAW that he had several weapons. Two pistols and two muskets, but what gained Cole's attention was a weapon with a large brass barrel. He pulled the weapon out to get a better look at it. It was a blunderbuss. A gun that he'd seen coach drivers carry, but never one so well kept. It was a beauty, in fact. The brass was a high quality and it had a lot of engraving. It was marked D-Egg London. Cole knew who Durs Egg was. The Earl said that he was without question the best gunsmith of his day. This particular gun must have been made for the army as it had a fold out bayonet.

"I've never seen you carry so many guns," Cole volunteered.

Joe smiled at his young friend. "That's because we will be carrying a large sum of money back," he said as he handed the horse's reins over to Cole. "Does that worry you?" Joe asked as he fumbled about and then, finally finding the right pocket, pulled out two cigars. "Care to try one?" he asked.

"Sure, but Sir William advised that I only smoke half a cigar until I get used to them."

"Good advice," Joe agreed, "only give me what you don't smoke. They are too expensive to waste."

Once the cigars were lit and drawing well, Cole spoke again. "I don't think Mr. Eriksson was happy that you won the fight, Joe."

"He wasn't," Joe answered. "He wanted me to, in fact, fake getting knocked out. He'd make a lot of money that way. He'd share it with me, of course. We'd then have a rematch and I could beat the sergeant in the first round. I told him that I'd think on it but decided my pride was worth more, especially doing what I do. I did say I'd play with the sergeant a few rounds, which I did."

"You played with him?" Cole asked. He thought it had been an all out fight.

"Aye, I did," Joe said, "and got my noggin beat good and proper for such foolishness. I decided that I'd get beat if I lay off any further so I took the fight to the sergeant."

"He was good, but not as good as it looked," Joe added.

"Does Mr. Eriksson owe you money, Joe? Is that why you are looking for him?"

Joe took the cigar from his mouth. "No, it was him that did poor Peg so badly."

"Are you sure, Joe?" Cole asked.

"Aye, I know in my own heart that he did it to get back at me for winning the fight."

"Can you prove it?"

"I will if I catch the sod. Peg made sure of that."

Cole remembered Peg's smile. "She was glad you came to see her, Joe."

"Aye, I told her she could rest easy as I planned to kill the whoreson."

They spent the night at a coach inn. Cole asked Joe, over their meal, about Covent Garden. "Have you ever gone to Covent Garden, Joe?"

"That's been on your mind for a time now, hasn't it Cole?"

Cole took a swallow of his ale, and then told Joe about Anne's penny novel with all the pictures.

"Aye, Cole. I was about your age when I first went. But there's naught there to compare with the lady you have in Deal. I'd not chance coupling with one of those wenches and catching a disease to take back. Besides, you've got to think of your future, lad. You can't go places in the army if your manhood is as big as a cannon barrel and dripping to boot."

Cole was laughing at Joe's description. "I have no desire to partake of the women there. I just want to see it and Drury Lane where the theaters are."

Joe smiled now, "If that's what you want, Cole, we can see both in an hour as they are close."

No more was said about Covent Garden but Cole did ask where they were going to get the money.

"Several London merchants buy goods from Sir George Aylward's agents, but no money ever changes hands." Before Cole could ask why, Joe added, "It would not be good business for a man who can't read, write, or do numbers, do collections as well."

"Do you always collect?" Cole asked.

"Not always. Eriksson does at times, but suddenly he's nowhere to be found."

CHAPTER TWENTY

JOE MADE HIS FIRST STOP just outside of London. This was at a large coaching inn. Joe handed the blunderbuss to Cole. "I want you to sit here with this in your hands. Put a scowl on your face and act like you're not afraid to pull the trigger."

The 'Old Kent Road' was a busy thoroughfare. People passed coming from and going to the city of London. They had made three stops with no difficulty. Joe put the money in a chest built onto the floor of the rig, each time. The fourth place was a pub and tobacconist called the Bear's Paw. Two men rode up as Joe went inside, tying their horses to a rack under a big tree.

Turning, one of the men pointed at Cole. "What ye got that ye need that old blunderbuss for, boy."

Cole did as Joe had instructed. He shifted in the seat so that both men were covered by the menacing weapon. "Move along," he said, as deeply as he could.

"You don't hardly look old enough to carry that gun," one of the men said.

Cole replied, his answer coming out of the blue, "This gun don't care how old the finger is that pulls the trigger. You two will be just as dead."

"Or worse, gut shot so it's a painful death," Joe said. He'd walked out and heard the exchange. He walked behind the rig, got in and took the reins to drive away. Once they'd got down the road, Cole put the gun down and took the reins so that Joe could put the money in the chest.

He turned to his friend after putting the money away. "That took nerve." After a pause, he added, "I liked what you said as well. It took those rogues by surprise too, I'm thinking."

"I was a bit scared," Cole said.

"You didn't show it and that's what matters. Of course, it would take a dumb man to go up against such a weapon," Joe said.

"Or a drunk," Cole added.

"Yeah, I agree with that," Joe said smiling.

***

STROLLING THROUGH COVENT GARDEN PROVED to be a disappointment for Cole. The brazen way the prostitutes flaunted their breasts on the street was far from appealing.

One poxed hag raised her short dress in front of Cole and shouted, "Take a look at paradise, laddy."

"More like hell," Cole responded as Joe pushed by her.

"What you see on the street, Cole, is those so poxed or used up that they can't work in the more upscale brothels, or so called coffee houses. Some of the most elite were called nunneries. One advertisement was particular disheartening as a madam was auctioning off some girl's virginity." Seeing Cole's look, Joe advised, "We've only another block or so of this, Cole."

"I'm glad," Cole answered. "This place sickens me, I've seen enough."

Drury Lane's theaters were more appealing. Fancy coaches and couples dressed for an evening's event lined the street. When Cole mentioned it, Joe nodded. After the shock of Covent Garden, he didn't want to tell Cole that some of those beautiful ladies dressed in the latest refinery were rich men's mistresses.

Joe hailed a hackney cab after passing the last theater, and they returned to Sir George's London flat. With the money they had just collected, Cole was surprised that Aylward didn't own an entire house.

"A flat is cheaper and less conspicuous," Joe advised.

The flat still had a full time maid servant and her husband helped when needed. The flat also had the advantage of being on the first floor, plus Sir George kept it well stocked.

Joe went to see Sir George's solicitor the following day, and delivered a thick leather bound folder. Once the proper receipts were signed, Joe took a cab to a bank named Thomas Coutts and Company. He had put on nice clothes this morning, putting away his travel attire as he conducted Sir William's affairs.

"I once heard a poem about Coutts Bank," Joe said smiling. "I believe it was written by Vere Carpenter." Clearing his throat, he straightened his coat and lifted his chin in mock importance.

"Money takes the name of Coutts
Superfluous and funny
For everyone considers Coutts
Synonymous with money."

Cole couldn't help but laugh, as much at Joe's mime as the poem.

The business at the bank took longer than Cole had expected. He and Joe were each armed with two pistols each as they entered the bank. Joe carried a chest that fit inside the chest built in the bed of the wagon. Two clerks carried the chest with Joe following them into a private office. The clerks returned soon after but Joe was in the office an hour before he returned. He was putting another leather bound folder in his coat when he returned through the door. Joe spoke to Cole as he walked toward the bank door.

"Our business is finished here. Would you like a meal in a fine restaurant or get an early start back?" It was not yet ten o'clock.

Cole's mind was on Linda and Anne. "We've eaten well since we've been here. I think sleeping in my own bed is more to my liking than food."

Joe smiled and thought, *aye, your own bed and likely Linda's as well.*

***

JOE WAS OF A MIND to stay at the coaching inn of Gus Harris. Gus had got his stake to purchase the inn by rowing an eight-man galley to Dunkirk and back. A musket ball from a Customs boat in the shoulder ended his smuggling days and nearly cost him his arm. His inn was aptly named the Galley Inn. The inn was near the town of Maidstone.

Maidstone was about halfway from London to Deal. The river Medway ran through the center of the town. When Cole and Phillip were younger, they spent several days visiting some of the Earl's relatives in Maidstone. During that time the boys had fished and gone boating in the river. The mention of the town brought back fond memories for Cole.

At times, Joe would lean from the wagon while driving down the road, and a few times he'd stop and look about.

"What is it?" Cole asked.

"I keep hearing the sound of horses, not on the road but in the trees. You'd better get that blunderbuss ready, Cole." Joe then looked at his young friend. "Cole, if men ride out of the woods with guns, it's not for a conversation." Joe let his words sink in. "Understand, Cole?"

"Aye," Cole muttered. He felt apprehensive. The thought of an armed man or men riding out with robbery and murder on their minds was enough to scare anyone.

An old coachman at Belcastle used to fill Phillip and Cole's heads with stories of highwaymen that he'd encountered on the coach roads. "Been wounded twice," the man said. "But I killed those who put a ball in me hide."

The old Earl, meaning Phillip's grandfather, had hung a man right there on the side of the road when he tried to hold them up. A note was pinned to his shirt for all to read…Highwayman. Those stories came flooding back to Cole's memory now. They did little to ease his anxiety.

They crested a hill and in the distance light could be seen. *This would likely be a spot*, Joe thought. Atop the hill, the highwaymen could see riders from either direction. If someone was coming, they could do their business and make their getaway into the forest. Joe was certain that they'd be well armed. Once they got the loot, they'd surely shoot both Cole and himself.

Joe had just cocked his pistol and placed it beneath his leg when two riders burst out of the woods, one from each side of the road. The suddenness of their arrival startled Cole. He'd been expecting them to come out way ahead, maybe blocking the road. Thinking of Joe's words, 'It's not for conversation.' Cole tilted the blunderbuss forward and cocked it. As he did so he wished for another weapon…a pistol, something to have on standby. There was still enough sunlight that the barrels of their pistols were visible in the riders' hands. The first rider's mistake was trying to stop the horse rather than paying attention to the men in the coach.

The rider's attention on the horses gave Cole more than enough time to bring the blunderbuss up and aim at the highwayman on his side. Cole didn't want to shoot a horse so he waited until the rogue was clear of the wagon's horse.

The rider on Joe's side was trying to get a bead on Joe with his pistol, when the still of the night was shattered by an orange flame and death spewed from the barrel of the blunderbuss.

Joe smoothly pulled his pistol from beneath his leg. He took aim and fired. His target grasped his chest and toppled off his horse. Joe clicked the reins and put the horse into a trot. There was little doubt that the sounds of the shots had carried. The explosion from the blunderbuss was enough to wake the dead. It would surely rouse the patrons out of the tavern to see what was afoot.

Several men were standing out in front of the inn. Joe, seeing his friend, called out, "Evening Gus."

Gus pushed his hat back and spat tobacco juice on the ground. "That be you, Joseph?"

"Are your eyes getting as bad as your arm?" Joe japed.

"They be growing dimmer," Gus admitted. He then added, "Thought we heard a cannon go off."

"That you did, Gus. It was my young friend here. It was high-waymen," Joe said. "We got past two but didn't stop in case there were more."

Gus called to two of his workers. "Take some torches and see what you find." He then turned to Joe and Cole. "We've hot bread, roast and potatoes. Oh...and as fine a ale that's passed ye lips."

"Convinced me," Joe said. Looking at Cole, he asked, "Sound good to you, Cole?"

"Absolutely, Joe, absolutely."

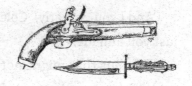

CHAPTER TWENTY ONE

PEOPLE WERE STARTING TO CALL the midday meal a luncheon. When it came to the luncheon, the Blue Post put on a spectacular spread. Fresh bread, several types of cheese, slices of beef or pork and a variety of sweet breads and pastries. Kimberly had her own chef but also a woman who was tops in cooking pastries. Coffee, tea, cocoa, small beer, and ale were available. Milk could also be had and there was a list of fine wines and sherry.

Cole had invited Anne and her parents to dine. Sir William had other commitments and couldn't attend. Cole was not really disappointed that he couldn't make it. Anne's mother, Mary, talked with Kimberly, who sat them at her table. With Mary talking to her friend, Cole was able to have a long conversation with Anne. She was as beautiful as any girl...woman he'd ever seen. He wondered if being away for a few days had made him more aware of her beauty. At one point in the meal, it dawned on Cole that Anne ate with her right hand but used her left hand to drink. *Do I do that at times,* he wondered.

"I have missed you," Anne whispered.

"And I you...greatly," Cole replied. "I wish that we could be alone, just you and me."

"Yes, but that might not be a good thing, Cole Buckley," Anne said. "You stir a fire in me that scorches my very soul."

"Aye," Cole said. "You do the same to me. If we were alone we may not be able to control the flames and the urges that I have for you. "

Anne looked at Cole, "I dream of us being together until the point that I want to tear off my clothes and give myself to you."

"What was that, dear, what about your clothes?"

Cole almost panicked but Anne was quick, "I said this food was so filling, I feel like I'm about ready to bust out of my clothes."

Anne's mother, Mary, smiled. "Yes, it is good."

While Anne talked to her mother, Cole saw Kimberly looking at him. Her gaze left little doubt in his mind that she'd heard the conversation. She'd keep her thoughts to herself, however. Would she tell Mary later? For some reason, Cole didn't think she would.

Cole went back to the tavern after the meal. He had told his uncle about the highwaymen's attempted robbery. He and Joe had talked it over. Joe felt there was little doubt the word would get back to Deal and his uncle at some point, so the best thing to do was to tell Angus about it to start with. That way it would be out in the open and if his father or the Earl were told, then Angus was already aware of it.

"Were you frightened, lad?" Angus asked.

"Yes sir, especially when the rogue pointed his pistol at me. In truth, Uncle, I didn't even realize that I'd pulled the trigger until the gun went off, giving me a great kick in my gut. It's still sore, in fact."

"Aye, lad, when ye fire such a weapon, ye need to make sure you've a firm grip on the gun. How about after, Cole, did it bother ye?"

"Some," Cole said, exaggerating a bit. "He was pointing the pistol at my face, so I knew it was him or me."

"Right ye are, lad. Never hesitate in such a circumstance." Placing his hand on his nephew's shoulder, Angus said, "Ye don't take time to talk when a man's intentions are obvious. Did the constable talk with ye?"

"No sir. He never came. Mr. Harris took the men's horses to pay for their burial but they didn't have anything else on them."

Angus nodded, "That's the way of it, lad."

Cole checked on Peg. She was sitting up and taking more nourishment. Sidney was full of questions about the shooting, and Dalton came by. Cole was happy with the way things were going. He'd been concerned about what his uncle would say or do.

He got a note from Linda saying she'd be up late that night if he were available. Marge had delivered the note. Cole just nodded his answer to the girl. Suddenly the barrels he was toting from the storeroom to the taproom didn't seem so heavy. The time did seem to drag on however.

***

COLE'S AUNT FLORENCE HAD PUT in for the entire family to attend church. Saint Leonard's was the parish church of Deal. The church was said to date back to the Saxon times. Cole wasn't sure what that meant entirely, but knew that is was a long time ago so the church was old. Cole realized it must be a special day, as they arrived. The yard was full of carriages.

Cole saw Sir William, Mary and Anne so he walked over and greeted them.

"It seems the word has gotten out," Mary volunteered. Seeing Cole's look, she added, "Our vicar is eighty years old today."

"It is a special day," Cole replied and meant it.

"Is there room in our pew for Cole, Father?"

Sir William looked annoyed at the question.

"I can sit with Uncle Angus and Aunt Florence," Cole countered.

"Nonsense, you can sit with us." Sir William still had a scowl on his face and Cole was about to decline when he realized that Anne's father was looking past him.

Cole turned and saw Sir George Aylward, and with him were a lady, a girl of twelve or fourteen, and a boy that may have been ten.

"I see that they've returned from Calais," Sir William snorted.

"William, we are at church," Mary hissed.

Anne leaned close to Cole and whispered, "Sir George's wife is French. They have a house and family in Calais." Cole nodded his head.

Sir William had been spoken to by his wife but he wasn't through. "There's no telling how much contraband he's arranged to be smuggled into Deal."

Cole saw his aunt and uncle and ran over to them. "I've been asked to sit with Anne," he told them.

"How sweet," his Aunt Florence said, while Angus just smiled.

A short service was given by the vicar. Afterwards much ado was made about the vicar's birthday. *He seems very energetic for an elderly man of eighty,* Cole thought.

Sir George's pew was across from Sir William's. Sir George's wife was very pretty and carried herself well. Cole wanted to ask Anne if she knew the children, but decided not to at church.

Cole felt a hand brush his shoulder as they were filing out of the church. He turned, catching a nod from Aylward...a nod and a smile.

When the Sunday services and festivities were over, Anne asked her parents if Cole could come over and go horseback riding.

"Not today I'm afraid," her father said. "I'm sorry, Cole, but I have business to attend to."

Anne crossed her arms and frowned. "It's Sunday. Why does Captain Letchworth have to come over today? He could come on Monday."

"Now, dear," Mary said, speaking softly but firmly. "Situations sometimes dictate that your father work odd hours."

Cole didn't want to be the cause of friction so he squeezed Anne's hand and said, "We'll get together soon." He was sure it was to defy her father, but as he turned to go she grasped his hand. Turning back around, Anne kissed him on the lips.

"Anne, you...you forget yourself," Sir William hissed.

"My apologies," Cole muttered.

"It's not your fault, Cole," Mary said as she took Anne's hand and led her to their wagon.

Sir William stood and glared at his daughter.

Cole was thinking, *God, I love you, girl, but you're going to get me shot.* As he was walking around the side of the church, he saw Joe helping Mary Stuart into a wagon, and spoke to them. Joe turned to greet his young friend.

"I'll not ask if anything is scheduled soon, Joe," Cole said, "but Captain Letchworth is meeting Sir William today."

This caused Joe to pause. He looked at Cole for a moment or so and then said, "Thank you."

As they made to leave, Mary invited Cole to join them for dinner one night soon.

"Be glad to," Cole said, meaning it. His stomach had growled each time he'd been to Mary's house and he smelled her baking.

***

COLE WAS MOUNTED AND RIDING later that night to see Linda. He had looked around the church that day but didn't see her. It dawned on Cole that afternoon how truly lonely the beautiful lady must be. She sent Marge to the baker and the butcher's shop. Saul did a little farming and took care of the livestock. She bought some produce from the Stuarts. He never saw her in town, other than the two late night visits to see him. He meant to see that changed...if he could.

While Cole was seeing Linda, Joe Lando sat drinking a brandy in Sir George Aylward's office. Joe explained that he didn't think the Monday delivery should go as scheduled.

"We can't cancel the merchandise," Aylward said. "We can change the place of the landing. It will mean a trip to Dunkirk for Lyons. He'll have to leave tonight. We'll land in Folkstone. Who will you send to see Crisp?"

"I think O'Hare. The two get along well."

Crisp was to Sir Alfred Munro, what Joe was to Aylward. There was little doubt Munro would consent to offer his men to unload Aylward's cargo. It would cost Aylward, but that was part of business.

"Do you think we might recruit young Buckley, Joe?"

"No!" The answer was short and firm. "He told me because he didn't want me to get hurt. I'll not see him put in any circumstance that would jeopardize his future. Besides, if too much didn't go as planned, it wouldn't be long before Sir William would suspect Cole."

"You care for the boy, don't you, Joe?"

"Aye, sir, with my life."

Sir George drained his glass of brandy and stood up. He took his cigar and placed it in the ashtray. The inch long ash falling before it got to the tray. "Who do you think tipped off Sir William?"

Joe didn't hesitate, "Eriksson."

Aylward nodded, "My thoughts as well."

"I didn't throw the fight, which cost him. I think that he shot Peg to get back at me, but she done him in with her nails. Had she not marked him and he'd killed her as he meant to, he would have been here tonight."

"I have never liked that Swede. He's good at what he does, so I used him, but I didn't like him."

Joe added, "Nor trust him, Sir George."

"No, never again. But he has little on me. I can always say I lent him money and he paid me back. He ran some errands for me, for which he was well paid."

"If it was him or you, Sir George, he'd make up enough to make life hard for you."

"Yes, he could do that. You intend to kill the man, don't you Joe?" Joe didn't answer but smiled. "Well, when you do, I'll take care of your alibi."

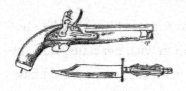

CHAPTER TWENTY TWO

FOR THE OWNERS AND PATRONS of the Cock and Bull, that Monday would long be remembered as a sad day. After it looked like Peg was making a good recovery and Doctor Garrett was pleased with her progress, she died. She apparently tried to sit up, as she was slumped over when she was found. She had spoken to Florence just before her lantern was blown out, and seemed to be doing better at that time.

Cole had caused two deaths, and they had not caused him any remorse. Peg dying filled him with despair, though. Was part of it because he'd turned her advances down? They had joked plenty of times about him being afraid of her. They had worked well together when Angus and Florence had gone to London. She was a girl who could flirt with every customer who walked in the door, but each one of them felt that that they were the one she really liked. Maybe that was it. Peg made everyone feel special, including him.

Cole felt a desire to kill, for once in his life; not in self-defense, but to avenge Peg. Killing didn't seem enough though. He wanted the woman's killer to suffer...to suffer so, that he'd pray for death.

The constable came back around and so did Sir William. They questioned Cole, Sidney and Angus again, looking for something that might have been left out. But they couldn't recall anything different.

When Sir William's coach was leaving, Sir George Aylward's coach came to a stop in front of the tavern. When he got down, Cole heard him address his wife as Andrea, and he called his children Luis and Amelia. They appeared like any other family, Cole thought trying to think of Sir George in Joe's light rather than Sir William's.

Angus was in the front of the tavern where the tobacco was kept and sold when Sir George walked up. "A word with you, Angus, if you've got the time."

"Aye, Sir George, please come in."

Sir George looked at Angus, then Cole, and back to Angus. "Do we need to go somewhere in private?" Aylward asked.

"No, Cole knows the basis in which we do business. I trust the lad completely."

Aylward nodded and then added, "It's your neck as well as mine." No reply was made to his comment but Cole did feel a lump in his throat.

"I've a few questions, Angus, and some not be shared."

Aylward didn't say with whom, but Cole felt he meant the constable and Sir William, the magistrate. "Do you feel Peg's attack had anything to do with our business?"

Cole spoke up first, "She was at the stable door, not the storeroom. I looked in there carefully as Peg and I rotated the last supplies that didn't come from London together." He cleared his throat, swallowed and said, "They were not in the stable at four a.m." No one asked Cole where he'd been. "That's why I checked the storeroom to see if there were any signs of them being in there."

"Good man," Sir George volunteered.

"The constable went to Peg's house, but nothing was amiss there. Betsy said that she hadn't seen her since early that afternoon before she was shot. She'd not been with a suitor at that time."

"Have you seen Mr. Eriksson around?" Aylward asked.

"Not since Joe's fight. He wasn't very happy when I last saw him," Cole said.

"You, Angus?"

"Ah dinnae ken," Angus said, slipping back to his Scottish sayings.

"He means that he don't know," Cole said as interpreter.

"If you recall or hear of anything, send young Cole to me right away."

Betsy called from the taproom, so Angus excused himself. When his uncle was out of hearing, Cole looked at Aylward.

"You think Eriksson killed Peg," he said.

"I've a suspicion," Aylward said.

"If he has claw marks where Peg got him, I'll kill the sod."

This was said with such vehemence that Aylward stepped back. *This one is a fire-eater*, he thought.

"You'll have to get in line, Cole. You know that Joe feels as you do."

"Aye," Cole answered. Another thought came to him then. "I'm not sure how I'd be received in some quarters were it known that I killed him." He said this dropping his head in anguish as he thought of Linda.

Aylward stared at Cole for a moment as if making a decision. "Don't be too sure that it would be met with hostility, Cole. There's some that feel that Matt being killed by the Customs men might have been a setup by his brother."

"Why?" Cole inquired.

"Maybe to open a path to his brother's wife. I'm told that both of the brothers had strong romantic inclinations toward Linda." Another thought occurred to Aylward, though he did not express it in front of Cole. *Peg's death may not have had anything to do with the fight and Joe. It may well have been Eriksson trying to get at his sister-in-law. To scare her into thinking he was not a man to be put off,*

Aylward had no doubt Eriksson wished it were he, and not Cole, who was sharing Linda's favors. He'd not mention it to Cole but he would to Joe.

***

SUPPLIES WERE DROPPED OFF THAT night in the back of the tavern. Included in the supplies were two hogsheads of leaf tobacco.

Angus called to Cole the next morning, "Put those two hogsheads of tobacco on the wagon and take them to Agnes. Sidney will show you where she lives. If Jacob is about, tell him that I've work for him today."

Cole picked up a crate of cigars that Agnes had rolled for his uncle, but Jacob was not about.

"I'll send the lad," she promised.

Cole took a leather pouch from his pocket and handed it to the woman. "Angus said this is for rolling the cigars."

Agnes smiled a toothless smile. "Be thanking your uncle for me."

Cole took an empty hogshead and put it in the wagon and left. Arriving back at the tavern, Cole took in the cigars as Sidney put up the wagon.

Betsy had brought a new girl to take Peg's place. Her name was Chloe. She was a pretty young girl who said she was eighteen, which was the youngest that Angus would hire. However, Cole didn't think that she was more than sixteen. He later mentioned it to his uncle.

"She'd not be more than sixteen, I'm thinking," Angus admitted. "Boot, would I rather she be here or at some bawdy house on Alfred's Square."

Cole thought about the madam at Covent Garden auctioning off her twelve year old daughter's virginity and agreed. "Where are her parents?" Cole asked.

"She says that they're dead. Betsy said her aunt kicked her out when she found her husband trying to bed her."

"It's good she's here," Cole agreed.

***

IT WAS AUGUST TWENTY-FOURTH, COLE'S birthday, and his father had sent word for him to come home. Angus loaded up the supplies he needed to take to Sandwich and with Cole on a horse and Florence and Sidney in the wagon, they made their way to Canterbury.

Once there, Cole was not surprised to see Major Samuel Huntington at Belcastle. Catherine was with him, but when she saw Cole ride up she dropped the major's hand and dashed over to Cole. Giving Cole a big hug and kiss, she took his arm and walked back toward the major. It pleased Cole to see she had the combs that he'd bought her in her hair.

"Samuel," she said, addressing the major. "I believe you've met my brother."

Major Huntington stuck out his hand. "It's good to see you, Cole."

Cole returned the greeting and asked, "Has my commission arrived yet?"

"It has been approved and I believe the funds have been sent. But with the reorganization going on, it will still be a while. If war is declared, it would get done much quicker," the major swore.

This caused Catherine to look disapprovingly at Huntington. "Sir, it sounds as if you prefer killing Frenchman than spending time with me."

"No, my dear lady, but it's coming. The sooner we can beat the Frogs, the quicker I can be back home at your side."

As Cole went to the back door, he thought he recognized a carriage, but it couldn't be. One of the maids saw Cole.

"Go on to your room. I'll get you some water to bathe in. Be quick though. Guests are already here."

Cole washed and dressed as quickly as he could. Leaving his room, he paused at the door to Phillip's room. *How he missed his friend...his brother.* He rushed on down the hall to the great room. He saw his mother first, but standing next to her was Mary, Anne's mother. Both women spotted Cole at the same time. When they turned, he saw Anne and she was talking to...damme, but it was Phillip. It was a grand birthday after all.

Anne saw Cole and rushed over and kissed him. He returned the kiss but nervously looked about the room. Thankfully, Sir William was in conversation with his father and Lord Bickford.

"I shan't kiss you like Anne," Phillip said, "but it's good to see you, Cole."

"And you, Phillip. Did you get my letters?" Cole asked.

"Every one that came before I left for Canterbury," Phillip replied.

"Doesn't Phillip look splendid in his uniform," Anne said, more a comment than a question.

"I will be wearing one of those before I'm finished," Phillip said.

Cole looked to where Phillip had indicated and saw Captain Best talking with Major Huntington. Catherine was walking toward Phillip, Cole, and Anne.

"How wonderful is this?" she asked her brothers. "We are all together again with Cole's beautiful girlfriend." Winking, Catherine leaned over, whispering to Anne, "You should hear the things that these two have done. I'm sure you'll change your mind about Cole."

Anne feigned surprise, "Maybe we should talk."

CHAPTER TWENTY THREE

PETER BUCKLEY WAS MORE THAN happy to show Belcastle's stables to Sir William. The Earl needed a few minutes with Captain Best, but promised that he'd join the men shortly. Once their fathers had gone to the stables, Anne asked to see the barn.

"Why?" Cole asked.

"I want to see where you and Phillip got caught peeping between the boards."

Cole flushed, "Catherine's got a big mouth."

Anne laughed, "Don't worry, Cole, I'm not angry. I've heard father say often enough that if a man don't look at a woman he's either blind or a sodomite."

Feeling a bit wicked, Cole pulled Anne to him, "I'm neither blind nor a sodomite, Anne." Holding her tight against him, Cole could feel the rise and fall of Anne's breasts against him. "The day will come when I will devour those breasts of yours."

"Oh, Cole, I look forward to that only...only I hope I don't disappoint you."

Cole put his fingers to Anne's lips to shh her. "I can promise you, Anne, you'd never be a disappointment to me."

Footsteps could be heard approaching. Anne quickly took Cole's hand and pressed it to her breast...to her heart. He could feel her heartbeat but as the steps grew nearer he moved his hand. It was Phillip, thank goodness, as he found himself getting aroused.

"I wondered if you'd be in the barn."

Anne smiled, "I understand the two of you had some fun times in this barn."

"Aye," Phillip smiled, not knowing what Cole had told her. "And some not so fun times when we got caught," he added.

Cole, Anne, and Phillip walked through the barn and down to a lake, shooing ducks out of the way as they neared the water. A couple of fish jumped, scaring Anne, as they were so close. She grabbed Cole's arm, and he and Phillip laughed. When Anne looked up, Cole bent his head and kissed her.

Phillip had a memory and said, "Cole, do you remember when we threw Catherine in the water?"

Cole laughed as the memory came back to him. Both he and Phillip turned to Anne. They quickly picked her up and swung her but didn't let go. They were both laughing, so she couldn't help but laugh also.

"I wouldn't speak to you for a month, had you thrown me in," she said.

"Have no fear, dear lady," Phillip said. "We got such a thrashing, we'll not likely ever do that again."

"Because it was a new dress," Catherine said. She and the major had walked up. "It was a beautiful dress with lace trim. The mud stained the lace and mother was furious. Not to mention my shoes."

Anne listened, understanding Catherine's anger. The relationship between these three was surely different than any she had ever known or heard about. When Catherine had said mother, she had to mean…Cole's mother. It was a unique situation indeed. But what if the Earl died? What would happen to Cole's family then? Had the Earl taken steps to insure that they'd be taken care of? Undoubtedly he had. But just in the time that she'd been there, she could see that both Phillip and Catherine seemed totally devoted to Cole's mother.

Walking back up, as they neared the top of the path, they saw Sir William with Cole's father and the Earl leading an Arabian dapple gray mare, but she was much darker than the usual gray.

"Peter picked her out as a foal," the Earl was saying.

"She is to improve our bloodlines," Peter said. "She is nearly two now, but the foals of a two year old are not nearly as large as when a mare is three. Their maternal instincts seem to be greater by that age as well. Watch this," he said.

Disconnecting the lead rope, he nodded to the men and they started to walk along the path again. Like a faithful dog, the mare followed along. At an intersection, Sir William and the Earl went right. Peter went left with the mare following him.

When they stopped for Peter to walk over to them, the Earl told Anne's father, "It's not just the mare; most of the horses will go to or follow Peter. You could have feed in your hand and they'd still go to him. King George, our premier stallion, will fight you over him. Peter caught a stable hand not doing as he'd been told and told the sod that he was fired. Not expecting an attack, Peter was caught off guard when the oaf shoved him down. King George charged the man with teeth bared. The oaf darted under the bottom rail of the stall or he'd likely been killed by the horse."

Peter chuckled at the narrative. "He never did come back to collect his pay, little as it was."

Seeing the men talk and laugh made Anne glad that they had come. She knew her father liked Cole but she'd heard his comments to her mother.

"We shall accept this invitation and see just how close young Cole's story is to the truth."

Her mother had replied, "William," in such a manner that Anne knew it to be disapproving.

Anne was somewhat fearful his story was not all true because of her father. Not that she cared. She'd marry him if he were no more than a fisherman...or worse in her father's eyes, an owler. The thoughts were dashed from her mind as one of the servant girls came to them and announced that dinner would soon be served.

Catherine took Anne's hand, leaned over and said, "That's Meg. She likes to show her wares and act the temptress."

"I'd fire her," Anne said.

"No," said all three males in unison, receiving glares for their comment.

***

THE RIDE BACK TO DEAL seemed to take less time. Partly because Cole's mind was preoccupied with the conversation that went on between Captain Best, Major Huntington, his father, and the Earl, as well as Angus. It was in regards to the impending war with France.

"Our fleet is down to nothing," Best moaned. "I'm lucky to have a frigate. I'm not a politician, but I can only wonder what they were thinking to lay up so many ships."

"It's the same with the army," Huntington said. "Our best officers have retired and most of our tough sergeants are out of the army."

"Not a few of which are making a living working as owlers," Sir William said.

Cole was glad that train of thought did not linger. The other reason the trip seemed to go fast was the horse Cole was riding. He was the son of Caesar, one of Belcastle's pure Arabian stallions.

The colt had not been named until Anne said, "Were he my horse, I would name him Apollo."

"Why Apollo?" Cole asked.

"He just looks like an Apollo to me," was her answer.

"A most beautiful gift, but not a horse you could put with other horses if we go to war." Major Huntington offered.

Peter spoke up, "Cole has several geldings of excellent quality. Apollo is to be his if he and Phillip do as they plan. That's to raise the best breed of horses in England."

"The world," Cole and Phillip had said in unison, causing the men to cheer.

Thinking back on that conversation, Cole felt a chill run through him. Hopefully, he and Phillip would survive, if war did come.

***

ANNE SPOKE TO HER PARENTS that night as the family prepared for bed. "This war with France is really going to happen, isn't it?"

Both of her parents stared at their daughter. She had been very quiet coming home. This was what was bothering her. Sir William looked at Anne. She was as smart as she was beautiful. He would not lie to her.

"Yes, I'm afraid it's almost certain," he said.

"There's a chance then that Cole...Cole and Phillip could die."

"There's certainly that chance," he admitted.

"You are going to have a young bride then, Father." Sir William and Mary were stunned.

"But Anne," Mary started.

"No, Mother, I don't intend for Cole to go to war without us making love."

"Has he made overtures in that direction?" Sir William asked.

"No, Father, he's too much the gentleman to do that." Sir William gave a sigh.

"We'll talk," Mary said.

"No, Mother, I've decided. With or without your consent," Anne replied.

***

JOE HAD LOOKED AFTER THE tavern while everyone had gone to Canterbury. He was standing in the door when they returned. He gave a whistle when he saw Cole on Apollo.

"That's some horse that you have there, my friend."

"It's a present from my father and his lordship."

"It makes my present seem small," Joe said. He stepped in the tavern and returned with a silver inlaid pair of dueling pistols.

"Oh, Joe," Cole exclaimed. "They are beautiful. I shall keep them on me when I report for my commission. Joe, you don't know what these mean to me."

"They're not a horse."

"No, but while that horse is at Belcastle, these will be by my side." Dismounting, Cole placed an arm around Joe. "Outside of Phillip, who is more my brother; you, Joe are my best friend."

Joe smiled, "You have another friend who asked me to tell you if you're not too tired after your journey, she'd think it kindly if you were to visit."

"That I shall, Joe that I shall."

Cole walked to the taproom after putting up Apollo. The new girl, Chloe, was busy trying to keep up with her share of the customers. She bent over once to pick up a coin and Cole saw most of her breasts. *She can't be any older than Anne, and maybe not that old,* he thought. And here she is working with a bunch of men, most of whom were already in their cups. She was better here than Covent

Garden, he acknowledged, but if he had a daughter, she'd never be forced to live so, he vowed...never.

***

COLE WAS ASLEEP, NESTLED AS he was in the arms of Linda. She had been a tigress that night. It was usually Cole who led the way but not that night. She wanted Cole to have a birthday that he'd remember and she'd succeeded.

Someone was at the door, Cole realized. Not just at the door, but they were pounding on it. Cole was up with his britches on when Linda roused up. Hearing the pounding on the door, she slipped on a robe.

Cole picked up one of his new pistols and walked behind her to the door, not wanting to create an embarrassing moment for her. When Linda opened the door, Saul was also there with a lantern.

"What is it?" Linda asked.

"We've a man that's been shot," he said. "A riding officer."

Cole wondered what time it was and looked at the standing clock. It was only a little after midnight. He still did not show himself but backed up when Linda said, "Help get him in, Saul, while I get dressed."

The two of them went back to her bedroom. Cole was worried about what his being there would do to Linda, and she was thinking the opposite. What would she do to his reputation?

"Slip out my window, and walk your horse down the lane before you mount him," Linda said as she pulled Cole to her and kissed him hard. As he hurried out the window, a voice inside her head said, *You'll go to hell for sure, for what you are doing with Cole.* Another voice inside her heart cried out, *I love him and it doesn't matter what people may say.*

CHAPTER TWENTY FOUR

T HE RIDING OFFICER DIED BEFORE Doctor Garrett got there. The constable was at Linda's by early morning, as well as Captain Letchworth and several of the preventive service men. Sergeant Duncannon's men were spread out.

One of the men called to the sergeant. Someone had been sitting on a rise overlooking the widow's house. They had been there long enough to have smoked two cigars. Duncannon sent a private to get Captain Letchworth. The captain returned and had the constable with him. Looking out over the area closely, it was obvious that someone had sat on the rise for a long time. In addition, to where they found the cigar, they also found where the horse had relieved itself, both from horse droppings and a still damp area on the ground where the horse urinated.

Captain Letchworth looked over the surrounding area. The trail led toward the cliffs and the Dover road in one direction, but from the evidence on the ground, it appeared whoever the murderer was had been watching the widow's house.

"Why shoot the riding officer then?" the constable asked.

"I would imagine the riding officer probably smelled the smoke and veered off his path to investigate," Letchworth said. "His horse or the murderer's horse might have given him away. Regardless, he should have taken better precaution."

"A big mistake," the constable said.

"That sort of talk will do his widow and children little good," Captain Letchworth responded.

The news spread quickly that another riding officer had been killed. The constable and Captain Letchworth rode to the tavern with one of the cigars. Cole had barely slept over concern for Linda. He was up early and done with breakfast when the captain and constable knocked on the door. Cole opened the tavern's entrance door.

"Morning, young sir," the constable said by way of a greeting. "We've a question for you."

Cole felt heaviness in his chest. Had they discovered he was at Linda's? It didn't matter to him other than what it might do to his relationship with Anne. He knew Letchworth and Sir William were close associates.

Before the constable could speak further, Angus called out, "Who is it, Cole?"

"The constable and Captain Letchworth, Uncle," Cole replied.

Angus hurried to the front, coffee cup in hand. "Would ye be coming in? There's coffee if ye desire."

"We haven't the time," Letchworth said. "I speak for myself, though."

The constable declined as well. "We stopped by to see if you recognize this cigar?"

"Yes," Angus said. "They are made in this shop...or for this shop, I should say."

"How can you tell?" the constable asked.

"By the manner and the feel of how it's rolled. A few other shops and pubs sell cigars but none of them have cigars rolled as fine as this."

The constable and Captain Letchworth nodded their heads. Angus then took a couple of fresh cigars that were different in length, but there was little doubt that they appeared to be like the one the men had found.

"Do you have a particular customer for these cigars?"

"No, we sell a lot of them," Angus smiled. "Most anyone that you can think of, and has the money to buy one, will have tried the cigar."

"Me included," Letchworth admitted. "I'm sure that the one Sir William gave me was one of these."

Sergeant Duncannon rode up outside. He walked in and saluted. "Sir, Campbell was a woodsman at one time."

"You mean a poacher," the captain corrected.

"Yes sir. He is of the opinion that the man was a lookout and not someone spying on the widow. He was looking around the house to see if the person had been closer. Well, sir, he found prints in the dirt where someone jumped out of the widow's window, ran to the stable and led a horse out. The tracks disappear in the woods so we don't know where they went or who it was. The corporal is riding to the constable's office now. I thought it best to bring her in as she refuses to answer any questions, sir."

"You did right, Sergeant, now ride to Sir William's house and notify him."

"Yes sir."

Cole, hearing this, rushed out the back to the stables and saddled Apollo. He ran the horse as fast as he could. He got to Sir William's house and flipped the reins over a hitching post and ran up the steps to the house. The maid opened the door and was almost run over.

"Where is Sir William?"

"In his office," the maid got out as Cole ran down the hall.

He entered the door in time to hear Sir William say, "I've long felt that she was in with the owlers. We'll make her talk."

"She wasn't with a smuggler," Cole shouted.

Sir William looked up startled and barked, "How do you know, Cole?"

"Because I was with her, sir."

Sir William stood staring, but from behind Cole came a gasp. "Oh no, how could you?" It was Anne and her mother.

She looked deep into Cole's face, "How could you? I loved you; and you said that you loved me. I hate you, Cole. Oh God, I hate you."

Duncannon stood there, his hat in his hands, looking dumbfounded.

Sir William looked at the sergeant, "Go tell Captain Letchworth to release the woman, and close the door on your way out." He went to a table and poured himself a drink. Sir William stood there for a moment, with the bottle in his hand, and then poured another drink, handing this one to Cole.

"I know what that cost you, Cole. You did the right thing but you've broken my daughter's heart. I know why you were there. I will even try to explain it to Anne. I will tell her you did it with my blessings to keep her pure. I'm not sure how much good it will do, though. Now, I have to ask you to leave and not return until I personally give you consent."

"May I try to talk to Anne, Sir William?"

"No!" Anne's father downed the drink in his hand, and Cole did likewise. "Should you write a letter. I will see that Anne gets it."

"Thank you, Sir William." Cole opened the door and Mary was there, her back against the wall. She had tears in her eyes. Her hand brushed Cole's sleeve, but she didn't speak.

Cole, walking Apollo back to Deal, met Dalton on the road. The young man stopped his horse and waited on Cole to get to him.

"I guess it's a bad time for you," Dalton said.

"You know?" Cole asked.

"The whole town knows by now. The dumb sergeant told what happened in front of the constable and his men. Word was spread by those loud mouths quickly. Your uncle was coming to see about you, but I asked him to let me."

"What are people saying?" Cole asked.

"You are a legend among the men I'd say, and the women think she's Satan's daughter. " Cole swallowed hard. "You are definitely a true friend, Cole. Not many people would have done what you did," Dalton swore.

Cole swallowed but didn't answer. Dalton touched his shoulder to let Cole know he felt for him.

Joe rode up just as Cole was getting to Deal. He looked at Cole but didn't speak. Joe was thinking, *it was me who put Cole and Linda together*. He also thought he knew who had killed the riding officer. He now had another reason to kill Eriksson, the sod.

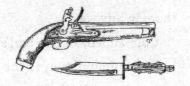

CHAPTER TWENTY FIVE

COLE WAS LEFT PRETTY MUCH alone when he got back to the tavern. His uncle, in his Scot's brogue, told him not to worry, things would work themselves out and to remember he had done the right thing. Aunt Florence gave Cole a hug while the new girl, Chloe, gave him a thorough appraisal.

"Peg was crazy about Cole," Betsy confided, "but he never took her up on any of her offers."

"Why would he?" Chloe asked. "Peg was a donkey compared to the widow."

"Don't you go speaking bad about me friend," Betsy warned.

"I mean nothing bad, Betsy, I'm just saying the widow has class." Betsy agreed with that.

Cole took a quill and paper to his room. He tried several times to compose a letter to Anne but he couldn't put words to paper. He did write to Phillip, then to his father, and lastly the Earl. The letters to his father and the Earl were basically the same letter. He told them the facts and then said he was sorry if he had embarrassed or hurt them in any way.

Cole added, in the Earl's letter, that if he wanted to withdraw his recommendation to the army, he understood and would find a way to repay the Earl for purchasing his commission. Cole had just finished his last letter when he realized that it had been quiet for the last hour. All the patrons had left the tavern. He was about to blow out his candle when his door creaked open.

Cole was startled till he realized it was Joe. Raising his hand in greeting, he motioned for Joe to enter.

"I've a lady who'd like to speak to you, Cole."

"Linda?" Cole asked. Joe nodded his head. "I'll get my coat."

"No, she's here," Joe said.

"Bring her in," Cole whispered, surprised at Linda coming to see him.

When Linda entered, she was dressed in men's clothing with a cape around her shoulders. He hugged her and kissed her cheek. Since there was only one chair, Cole walked her over to the bed. He had felt the wetness on Linda's face where she had been crying. His heart went out to this woman. *Why...*

"Why did you do it, Cole?" she asked.

"To protect you," he answered. "I couldn't let them hurt you...I love you, Linda. You mean far too much to me, to see you humiliated and questioned by Sir William. He can be ruthless."

"But it's cost you, Cole."

He didn't have a comeback for that other than to say, "It was the honourable thing to do."

It was awkward sitting as they were, so Cole pulled Linda down on the bed. He kissed her face and eyes, and held her close to him. Linda moved her head until she was comfortable in the crook of Cole's arms.

She'd never had anyone, including her husband, go to such extremes for her as Cole had. He had a way about him. She felt safe in his arms...she felt contented. She would not have sex with him again...not if she could prevent it. She wanted him, wanted him badly right now. But the best thing she could do for Cole would be to put distance between them. She would write Anne also, and take some of the blame off of Cole if she could. If the girl didn't respond, she'd strangle her and take Cole back to her bed and damn all of England if they didn't like it.

***

A WEEK HAD PASSED SINCE the night Linda had come to his room. He had awakened and realized that she was gone. Joe had stopped in for a tankard and asked Cole if he had time to continue his fighting instructions.

Cole smiled, but then his face turned sad. "I've don't have Anne or Linda to occupy my time so I have lots of it." He then turned serious. "How is Linda doing?"

"I don't know, Cole. She left the day after she visited you."

"Where?" Cole asked.

"I don't know."

"I stopped by and Saul just said that she'd left, but didn't say where."

Damn, Cole thought. "Maybe it would have been better for her had I not spoken out."

"No, Cole, what you did was right."

Cole thought, so she is gone. She might have left but she'd never be forgotten."

The next day Cole got two letters, one from his father and the other one from the Earl. He opened the Earl's letter first, for some reason.

Dearest Cole, my son,

You have given me nothing to be embarrassed about. You have done nothing every young man your age hasn't done or wanted to do. You, at least, showed good judgment by not dallying with some married woman, or worse, some poxed, bawdy house wench. That would have caused me concern. You chose a woman, not some girl who didn't know what she was doing, to have a liaison with. And when the lady was about to have her character questioned, you rose up in her defense. A most honourable and noble action if you ask me. I would hope that Phillip would act just as honourably. So put your mind at rest, Cole. I put no shame on your actions. Just pride in the fact that you behaved as a man should.

I remain your servant,

C.B.

The letter had not been signed with all the trimmings most of the Earl's letters carried. Other than the stationery, some might not even recognize it as the Earl's, but Cole did. His father had said similar things, only he addressed Cole's feelings and how he was sorry that he'd gone through all he had.

After reading the letters, Cole picked up the ink well, quill, and paper and wrote Anne a letter. He felt like he could find the words now. He knew that her parents would likely read the letter, so he had to be careful how he worded it.

My Dearest Anne, my Love,

I write you this letter not to try to persuade you to forgive me. That may never be possible. But as I stood before your father and told the truth to him about the widow, you should you realize I don't lie. So having reinforced that simple fact, I want you to know that I truly and with all my heart love you. If I thought it would change your feelings, I'd have Phillip's bosun take his cat and lay it on until you said stop. I didn't go to another woman's bed because I didn't love you. And as improbable as it may I did it because I loved you. Being around you is like a furnace to my soul. A furnace so hot it was boiling over. I gave your father my oath that you'd be as pure as snow when we married. Therefore, I found a means to quench those flames. Should you decide you have no wish to see me again, I understand. It's been pointed out to me that had I kept my mouth closed you'd never have found out about my transgression. But that's not the type of man I am. You may hate me and you have the right to. But at least you know I don't lie or sidestep responsibility. I will always love you.

Your servant,

Cole

Cole folded the letter and addressed it to Anne. He then found Sidney. "I've a chore for you."

"Doing what?" Sidney asked.

"I want you to take this letter to Sir William's house. Give it to Anne, her mum or Sir William. Do not leave it with a servant. You can ride Apollo and when you get back, I'll give you a shilling." Sidney reached for the letter. Cole continued, "Go saddle Apollo, and then wash your hands, put on a presentable coat and then come get the letter."

After spending an hour fighting for his life, that afternoon, Cole was glad when Joe called it a day for their training. The man was a demon when it came to fighting and he'd not gone all out with Cole. Not even close.

"You are learning, Cole," Joe said. You've caught on to a number of the more common defenses but you still lack the killing drive. Maybe your mind is on that girl. I don't know but if you go to war, it damn well better be on staying alive."

"I...I don't want to hurt you, Joe."

Joe laughed, "You hurt me!" He might as well have spit in Cole's face.

Cole attacked with a fury. When Joe finally had him subdued, he said, "That's it. That's what I want from you every lesson. Don't think of me as your friend. Think of me as your worst enemy. Think of me as the one who has just raped your mother. Fight fiercely but don't let anger get you in trouble. Anger makes a man make mistakes."

Cole smiled. His fencing instructor had said the same thing.

Cole and Joe went round after round for the next several days. Cole was to the point that he was actually getting to Joe occasionally. Sidney had watched and when they finished, he went to get them a tankard.

While Sidney was in the tavern, Cole asked, "Has there been any word about Eriksson?"

"Not a word, Cole."

"Joe, do you think that might have been him watching to see who was at Linda's?"

"I didn't want to mention it, Cole, but that's exactly who I think it was. Had the riding officer not come along, it might have been you with a ball in your gut."

"When I saw those cigars, he was the first one that I thought of," Cole admitted.

Sidney came out with the tankards and Joe flipped him a coin. "For you, lad."

Thank you, Joe." Sidney, feeling that he owed Joe a favor, walked closer. "I heard Chloe say that she'd love to find out if you were as good with your wedding tackle as you are with you fists." Joe cuffed Sidney playfully.

"Tell Chloe that Joe's about to be a married man," Cole said.

With his shirt off, Joe had the build to draw women. No wonder the girl was being forward. It was unlikely that she'd see another man built like Joe.

Cole took a bucket of water from the well and dumped it over his head. He heard Joe saying, behind him, "You have company, Cole."

Cole turned around drying his face. When he let the towel drop, he saw Anne standing there. She looked at him and then ran to him, hugging him to her. Cole hugged her back and kissed her long and hard. He pushed her back a bit.

"I'm wet. It will ruin your dress."

"I don't care," Anne said, and then pulled him to her once again, kissing Cole long and hard, and not caring who was looking. She had her Cole and that was all that mattered.

Sir William Brabham smiled, standing at the corner of the tavern. His daughter was happy again, so little else mattered. Besides, he liked Cole...damned if he didn't.

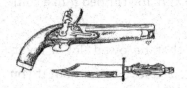

CHAPTER TWENTY SIX

"CALAIS...CALAIS, FRANCE."

"Yes, Cole. Do you want to go?

"Yes, when would we leave?"

"Wednesday."

Cole was thinking. Today was Sunday and he'd been invited to Sir William's that afternoon. "I will ask Uncle Angus and tell Anne that I might be gone a few days," he said.

"You'll know tomorrow then?"

"Yes," Cole answered Joe.

While riding with Anne and her parents, Cole brought up the subject of his possibly accompanying Joe to Calais. They would be escorting Sir George's wife and children to her mother's for a visit. When they returned they would be bringing Andrea's mother back with them. Andrea had gotten a letter from her brother fearing for their mother's life.

Sir William thought for a bit and then said, "I think it would be fine, Cole. I don't think that even the most black-hearted smuggler would put his wife and children at risk trying to bring back smuggled goods." After a pause, he added, "I understand people in France are convinced that with Napoleon Bonaparte as head of the government, he will not rest until he's either conquered the world or dead. I shouldn't wonder Sir George would want to get his wife's relatives out of France along with anything of value."

Anne who was riding beside Cole holding his hand asked, "Why must you go, surely there are others who could do this?"

"I'm sure there may be some who can do it better," Cole said. "It's just that Joe trusts me to maintain a level head and not act unless it's absolutely necessary. Others may act to quickly and cause damage when a level head would not."

"If you must," Anne said, "but I don't like it and I'll not rest until you are back."

✳✳✳

COLE, ALONG WITH JOE, ANDREA, and her children boarded the lugger Alert. The lugger had six crewmen on board.

"A small crew to make room for Sir George's family," Joe whispered to Cole.

The captain and crew of the lugger knew what they were doing when it came to handling their vessel. It was just before noon when the captain reduced sail to enter the port of Calais. Cole turned toward the stern and for a moment could see the cliffs of Dover.

"I didn't realize we were so close to England that we could see the cliffs," Cole commented.

"Aye," Joe responded. "It's a bit further to Deal though."

Once the ship was tied up, the captain and a mate went ashore. It was close to a half hour before he returned with a Frenchman.

"I have arranged transportation for you and the children," he said. "I'm sorry that it's not a carriage."

Cole and Joe walked closely behind as the captain led the way back. About halfway, Joe scooped up Luis and carried the small boy on his shoulder, as the little man was starting to lag behind. A French officer with a platoon of soldiers was walking near where the wagons waited. Joe looked at Cole. They were both hoping that trouble would not start so soon. The recent French Revolution had cost a good many of the French aristocrats their property, if not their lives. Those in the officer corps now were not the gentlemen their predecessors had been.

Andrea and the captain spoke to the lieutenant, as did Luis. Cole was not sure what was said, but it made the lieutenant and his soldiers smile.

Andrea paused, once they were at the wagon, "Luis told the lieutenant that he was going to see his grand-mére, which means grandmother."

I'd smile too, Cole thought. He hadn't realized it at first, but the part of Calais they were in appeared to be an island with a fishing village. The wagon trip to Andrea's mother did not take long. Her brother, Henri, showed relief at seeing his sister.

There'd been no executions in Calais, but there had been an increased number of army troops, and a couple of fishermen said they'd been stopped by guard boats.

Andrea's mother was not as alarmed or worried as her son. Still, a few boxes of her most prized possessions had been packed up to take back to England.

After understanding that Joe was Sir George's main lieutenant, Henri pointed out where chair legs had been hollowed out and gold was melted and poured into the legs.

Joe said, with Andrea relaying his words to her brother, "The only problem is it now takes two men to lift a chair that one person should have been able to move easily."

The chair legs were broken apart with the time that they had, and the gold was taken out. Joe found a bit stock and bits in the back of their house. He bored holes in the legs of three other chairs. The gold was melted down again and divided up between the three chairs.

"I'd bring the chair with the broken legs," Cole said. "If we are stopped it will look better having all four chairs. We can say Sir George is going to have a carpenter make new legs so that they all match."

Everyone agreed this was a good idea so when the wagon was loaded, the four chairs were included. Henri drove his mother and sister back to the port while Joe, Cole, and the children followed in the wagon.

When they left, the French lieutenant asked Luis if he saw his grand-mère. The boy smiled, repeating what he'd been told. "Oui, nous emmenons grand-mère en vacances," meaning we are taking grandmother on a holiday. The lieutenant smiled, waved and said "amusez-vous," meaning 'have fun'.

Due to the time boring out the chair legs, re-melting and pouring the gold, Alert left a couple of hours later than planned. Alert's captain grumbled and said that he had been ready to up anchor without them.

Joe's face grew stern. "I'd think that Sir George would not take it kindly you departing in his boat and leaving his family." He knew the captain hated for Alert to be called a boat so he did it to antagonize the captain.

The sun had finally slipped over the horizon and Alert was almost to the Downs when a boom was heard and a ball splashed not far ahead of them.

"A Customs boat I'd think," the captain swore. "They think we're a smuggler."

Joe nearly laughed out loud. At any other time, that was exactly what the lugger was used for.

"Heave to," the captain shouted his order.

The lugger's sails quickly came down. The revenue cutter, Swallow, was soon alongside. Grapnels were tossed and the two ships were pulled together. Cole was quick to see that before the cutter's captain came on board, swivel guns were aimed at the lugger. While a lantern had been lit aboard the lugger's stern, as the sun went down, several more were lit so that the women and children were clearly visible.

The cutter's captain stepped on board the lugger asking, "What ship is this?'

Cole thought that was a dumb question as the name Alert clearly hung on the stern.

"She's the lugger, Alert, and I'm Captain Isaiah Barnes."

"She's your ship?"

"Aye!"

"She doesn't have the smell of a fishing vessel."

"Nay, I hire her out mostly for transporting."

"Transporting smuggled goods I don't doubt," the Customs officer replied.

Joe stepped forward at this time, "And your name is, Captain?"

The captain didn't answer Joe but asked, "Who are you?"

"I'm the person who hired this vessel," Joe responded without giving his name. He then pointed to Cole and said, "That's the Earl of Belcastle's ward...er, son more likely."

It dawned on Cole that his being aboard had been planned for just such an occasion. He took a breath and took a step forward. "I say, Captain, have you by chance been to Portsmouth of late?"

"Why no! Why would you ask?"

"My brother is a midshipman on the Diamond 38, Captain Best. Were they in port I might have Captain Barnes take me to Portsmouth."

"I'm sorry, I wish I did know," the captain said.

"And what's your name?" Cole asked.

"I'm Stephen Mitchell."

"It's good to meet you, Captain. Now, if you've no more to do we should be on our way. I promised our guest that we'd be home for dinner. I'm sure Anne, Sir William Brabham's daughter will be very angry with me."

"You vouch for this ship and her captain?"

Cole looked at the man. "How can I vouch for what I don't know, but I don't believe my man, Joseph, would have allowed us to board a vessel that was carrying on unlawful activities with us on board."

"I'd think not," Captain Mitchell replied.

Cole called to the captain as he was leaving, "Should you be in Canterbury some day, please stop by Belcastle for refreshments."

"I shall," the captain said.

"Hopefully it will be soon," Cole added, "as I've been given a commission in the Prince of Wales Own." The captain nodded and saluted.

Joe came to Cole once they were underway. Cole glared at him, "You used me, Joe. You thought we might be stopped and knew that with my name and connections I could get us by."

"Cole, I..."

"Don't say anything, Joe. I would have risked my neck for you. And this is how you used our friendship."

Joe tried to speak again, but Cole turned and walked forward. Joe gave a sigh and, turning aft, he found himself face to face with Andrea.

She had an angry look on her face. "Did George put you up to this, Joe?"

Joe went to walk around her but she grabbed his arm and pulled him around to face her. "He did, didn't he?"

Joe dropped his head but didn't answer. To her that was answer enough.

"We don't have many true friends, Joseph Lando, and I fear that you've just lost the best one you've ever had," Andrea said, still fuming.

With his head still hanging, Joe asked, "Is that all, Madame?"

"For now," Andrea replied.

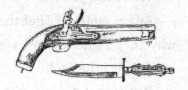

CHAPTER TWENTY
SEVEN

JOE RARELY SET FOOT IN the tavern over the next six weeks, other than on the nights when they were landing smuggled goods. Angus noted there was a coolness between his nephew and Joe, but Cole didn't desire to discuss it.

There were three landings of smuggled goods that were evident by either Joe or Paddy O'Hare showing up at the tavern on the nights the landings were scheduled.

Cole said to his uncle after the tavern closed on a landing night. "These revenue men must have shat for brains. All they'd have to do was watch the taverns to know when a cargo was landing."

"That much is true," Angus replied, "but the ships usually land when it is the darkest at the preset locations. Spotsmen on board might send a spark from a tinder box or a flash from a flintlock pistol without a barrel. This produces a very distinctive blue light. On the beach, a land party would return the spark if it was clear. If they thought a Customs or revenue man had sent the signal the real beachman might build a bonfire or light a beacon."

"The smugglers have it figured out, don't they?" Cole remarked.

Angus smiled, "That they do, and still some get caught. That's why they fight so hard when they are caught. If they don't get hanged, it's the gaol.

"Who's to take care of their families then?" Cole asked and then said, "You have a great knowledge of it, Uncle."

Angus stared at Cole for a moment. "If you live on the coast of Kent, you'd better if you want to get by."

The first week after Cole had returned from his trip to Calais, he'd gotten a letter from Andrea Aylward. She expressed her sorrow, in the letter, at Cole having been used by her husband. He'd felt with Cole along there'd be less likelihood of danger to her, her mother, and the children. She asked him to be mad at them, yes, but poor Joe hadn't realized what he'd done until Cole had spoken to him. He'd had harsh words with her husband, saying that at the end of the year he was through.

Cole wondered if that was possible. Things had returned to normal with him and Anne. Their kissing had been toned down by Anne, and at one point she let it slip that she'd gotten a letter from Linda.

Linda had taken a lot of the responsibility for her and Cole's lovemaking but added that Anne had his humours so inflamed that he was about to explode. She explained that men could not just turn off the desires like some women did. She had said that while Cole was indeed a healthy man, Anne had actually driven Cole to her bed so that her virginity would be protected. She'd ended the letter saying she was not sorry that she'd bedded Cole, no woman would be. But if one chose to light a fire, they'd better be ready to put it out or someone else would.

Cole was very surprised to hear about the letter. But while parts of it were true, not all of it was. He'd sought Linda's arms without having been around Anne, many a night. He didn't mention it, of course, thinking some things were better left unsaid.

***

THE NEWS WAS TRAGIC. COLE had a sinking feeling in his chest. Last night after the landing, Joe was shot taking borrowed horses home. He'd been shot in the back and left lying on the road. It had not been a riding officer or duty man. They would have gotten help and brought Joe in.

No, this was some black-hearted murderer lying in wait for Joe. If his horse and the borrowed horses had not made some noise running into John Stuart's yard, Joe might have died. Stuart knew that things were not as they should be, so he took a lantern and went out to check. He found Joe's horse quickly enough and there on the saddle was blood...a lot of blood. Stuart had called for Mary to hitch up the wagon and follow him as he searched. Stuart was kneeling over Joe when Mary got there. He'd been shot high in the back and was unconscious. They had dressed the wound, and then with Mary in the back of the wagon with Joe, they went to Doctor Garrett's.

When Cole went for breakfast, Chloe was already there. She said lots of people were out on the street talking about Joe.

"What about Joe?" Cole asked. When told he rushed through breakfast and then ran over to the doctor's.

Joe was bandaged up and laying on some pillows. Cole walked over to him and no one tried to stop him. Mary looked up and smiled at her man's friend. She was glad that he came, knowing what they'd been through.

Cole took Joe's hand and gave a slight squeeze. "You get well soon, Joe Lando, we've lessons to finish." Joe didn't speak but gave Cole's hand a bit of a squeeze. "We are here for you, Joe...we all are," Cole said speaking softly.

Joe was soon asleep and Doctor Garrett told everyone but Mary to leave. The constable was outside when Cole came from the house.

"Have you been to where Joe was shot?" Cole asked.

"Not yet."

"I'll go get my horse and we'll ride out together," Cole said, leaving the constable no room but to accept.

"Mary said they found Joe in the lane just past where you would turn off to go to Linda's house," the constable said.

Cole thought, I wonder if Eriksson is still hanging around. When he met up with the constable he mentioned it might be good to check in at the widow's, after they looked over the area where Joe had been shot.

"The widow is gone," the constable said.

"Saul's there," Cole countered.

The spot where Joe fell off his horse was plain. The weeds were broke off and there was blood, most of it dry by now. After seeing where Joe fell, Cole and the constable tried to figure out where the shooter might have been. There were only a couple of likely spots.

Walking back and forth as he would, looking for blood from a wounded buck, Cole soon found where the rider had been when he shot. Unlike when the riding officer had been shot, it appeared Joe's assailant had followed Joe until he could get a good shot and took it. However, like with the riding officer's shooting, a cigar butt had been thrown on the ground. Cole picked it up and handed it to the constable.

"It's not the same kind as before but a cigar all the same," the constable said.

Cole suddenly wished that he'd paid attention to see if a cigar had been in the stable the night Peg had been shot. Mounting up, they rode up the lane to where it went to Linda's house. Cole saw that a wagon had been down the lane recently. I wonder if she's back, he thought to himself. It came to him then that Doctor Garrett might have been visiting Marge.

Saul came to greet them as they rode up. While the constable was explaining why they were there, Cole couldn't help but think back on his times there with Linda, fond memories. Suddenly he saw a curtain move. It was quick but it moved just the same. His horse blew, and then stomped its front foot. Cole, without realizing it, had gripped the reins tighter than he meant to. Saul was saying the horses had been uneasy late last night but after he didn't see anything, he thought it might have been a fox or something.

"We will get on back to Deal," the constable said. "Let us know if you hear something." Saul replied that he would.

Cole purposely dropped a glove on the ground. He pulled up down the lane a bit and swore. "Damme, I've dropped a glove. I'll be right back." Turning Apollo, he hurried back to Linda's house.

Saul heard the horse and turned around. Cole rode over to where the glove lay. "I dropped my glove." Saul picked it up for him.

"Saul, I know someone is in the house, probably Linda," Cole said. "I think Eriksson is about and it's just as dangerous for her as anybody. So keep your gun handy. Shoot first, Saul. He's evil." Saul nodded, and then Cole added, "Tell Linda I said thanks and I'll never forget her."

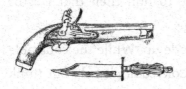

CHAPTER TWENTY EIGHT

EOPLE LOITERED AROUND DOCTOR GARRETT'S office for days hoping to hear how Joe was progressing. Joe was the kind of man who was quick to lend a helping hand without expectations. He was Deal's own bare knuckle champion. So what if he was involved in the free trade. Who along the coast wasn't unless you were the magistrate or a Customs man? Some of them had their purses fattened by those that were.

The man who shot Joe was an unpopular scoundrel as any could be. Doctor Garrett had to limit the number of visitors that Joe could have. The exceptions were Mary and Cole. On one visit, Cole was accompanied by Anne. Joe seemed to like this and flushed when Anne gave him a kiss on the cheek as they left. One other time Joe tried to apologize to Cole about the trip to Calais. Cole shushed him and told him that it was forgotten.

Three weeks after Joe was shot, he was placed in a wagon and taken to the Stuarts. Sir George had Paddy O'Hare and a group of armed men escort the wagon. If that was not enough, a round the clock guard was set up.

When asked if danger was still suspected, Paddy replied, "Who knows, but Sir George isn't taking chances with the champion of Deal and all of Kent."

This was enough for most, but Cole felt that it went deeper. Joe was a big part of Aylward's smuggling operation. Cole looked at it as Sir George protecting his enterprise. The morning that Joe was taken to the Stuarts, Sir George's wife carried a basket full of things she knew Joe liked. Cole was a bit surprised, but Deal was a small town. Everybody knew everybody. Knowing what a good Christian woman Andrea was, Cole realized that he'd have been more surprised if she hadn't done something. Andrea, he decided, was a better person than her husband.

The search for the killer of Peg and the riding officer had thus far come up empty-handed. Cole felt it was the same person who had tried to kill Joe and he felt it was Leif Eriksson. Cole decided that he'd not leave it up to the constable and his men. He was going to do some checking himself.

***

IT WAS A TUESDAY NIGHT and the tavern was filling up. "Must be a landing tonight," Angus whispered to Cole. That thought was driven home when Paddy O'Hare came in.

He walked to the bar instead of going to his usual back corner table. "It's good I caught you together," Paddy said. "We are going to be busy tonight and I'm short-handed."

This confirmed Angus' earlier comments. Cole was expecting the Irishman to request either one or both of them to help with the landing of supplies. Paddy did ask for help but of a different sort. "Being short-handed, I'm going to have to pull my men watching over Joe. Do you think you might be able to fill in for the evening?"

"What time?" Cole asked, realizing his mistake. "I mean when do you want us in place?"

"About the time you'd close, I'd say. I think your customers should be gone by eleven p.m."

"The girls can clean up," Angus said. "I'll have Cole gone as soon as the crowd thins out, and then head out later myself."

"God be with ye, Angus, my friend. I wouldn't be letting on to the wenches what's afoot."

"Paddy," Angus said, gripping the Irishman's arm. "There's naught to worry about from those in my employ."

Paddy smiled, "I know that, Angus, it's just a habit of late. Not only do we have the duty men to worry about, there's some amadan that's got my men constantly looking over their shoulders and not moving their arses in a timely manner." He shook hands with Angus and Cole. "It's good men, ye are."

Cole asked, once Paddy was out of hearing, "What's an amadan?"

"That's Irish for idiot or fool."

Cole nodded his head. "Why didn't he just say idiot or fool?" Angus shrugged his shoulders.

The ride out to the Stuart farm caused memories to flood back as Cole rode past the lane to Linda's house. He was tempted to ride down the lane to make sure all was well. Who do I think I'm kidding, Cole admitted to himself. It's Linda I want to see...and not for polite conversation. He kicked Apollo into a faster gait, wanting to get past the turn off as quickly as possible before his desires overrode his best instincts.

He was through the gate to the Stuart farm when a man rode from between two trees.

"It's you, is it?"

"Aye," Cole responded, not knowing what else to say.

"I was supposed to stay until you arrived."

Cole threw up his hand in salute as the rider put his horse into a lope. Through the cracks in a closed shutter, a light shown from the house. Cole went to the door and knocked.

A voice...Mary's...,"Who is it?"

"It's me Cole, Mary. I just wanted to let you know I'm here."

"Thank you," Mary said. "I'll get you some coffee."

Cole could hear Mary stirring around in the house, the clang of the coffee pot, and soft whispers, barely audible conversation. After a moment, the door creaked as it was opened. It was Mary with the coffee but behind her, moving slowly, was Joe.

Cole stood up to give Joe a hand. "Should you be out here?"

"No, he shouldn't, Cole, but he's as stubborn as any man I know."

Cole helped Joe into the chair that he'd been sitting in and got another one from the far end of the porch. Splinters flew from the chair as he turned. A shot had been fired, with the impact knocking Cole down. He quickly rose up and darted to where Joe and Mary were. They had both gotten down on the boards.

"Your horse obstructed his view," Joe said with harsh breaths. "When you moved, he had a clean shot."

"I'm tired of this," Cole swore.

He quickly untied Apollo's reins and then swung up on his back. Riding low on his horse's neck, he charged up the hill towards where the shot had come from. Another shot was fired. Cole didn't feel or hear the ball passing but he did see the flash from the barrel. He angled Apollo more toward the flash. He saw a rider mount a horse. He took a shot with his pistol, knowing it was too far for an accurate shot. He did see the rider duck down. Out of the trees now and on the Dover Road, Cole pushed Apollo to an all out gallop.

They were closing now and Cole took out his second pistol and attempted another shot. Had he missed? The fleeing rider's horse veered to the left when he shot. Cole was even closer now. He'd soon be on the rogue. The rider surprised Cole as he swung his horse off the road and down a worn path. It was a path that led to the cliffs.

Cole had fallen back a bit now, not knowing the path. As he rounded a sharp bend, another shot rang out. Cole heard the buzz this time, as the ball passed near his head. The shooter had dismounted, leaving his horse. Cole pulled back on the reins, bringing Apollo to a skidding halt. He hated losing sight of his quarry but both of his pistols were unloaded. Staying down and using the rogue's horse for cover, Cole quickly loaded both pistols. Taking a chance to look around the horse, Cole could see a fleeing man headed down a path toward the edge of the cliffs. Just as he ran passed the shooter's horse, he saw where the man had dropped a musket. Reaching over, Cole grabbed it.

Cole went as fast as he could, not knowing the winding path, but that was not as fast as the fleeing man. They were now at a point that Cole could see the man clearly below him. Taking a chance, Cole pulled the musket to his shoulder and fired. Did he hit the man...he wasn't sure as his shot triggered off several shots, the balls passing damnable close. He dove to the ground amid shouts and curses.

One of the voices he thought he recognized. "Captain Letchworth," he called...and then called again. "It's Cole Buckley, Captain."

Several uniformed men surrounded Cole, within a few minutes, and disarmed him.

"I was chasing the shooter," Cole tried to explain.

"Shut yer bleeding mouth or I'll be bashing ye," a corporal snarled. "Ye about took me head off with that shot."

Cole said, not liking the man, "I doubt it. I'm not that good a shot."

The corporal drove the musket butt into Cole's stomach doubling him over. Gasping, Cole said, "One day you'll regret that."

The corporal drew his musket back for another blow but a voice rang out in the darkness. "That's enough, Smyth."

"We got us one of the scum, Cap'n. 'E fired a shot at me."

"You liar," Cole snarled. "It's me, Cole Buckley, Captain."

"Hmmm, light a torch, Anderson."

"But the smugglers, Cap'n."

"With all those shots, do you think they're still around?"

"It was 'e what set off the alarm," Smyth accused. Cole just glared at the idiot.

A torch was lit and Letchworth could see that it was Cole. "What are you doing out here, Buckley?"

"As I tried to tell this ...this idiot, Captain, I was chasing the shooter. He shot at me at the Stuarts' house, and several more times on the road. He left the road and got off of his horse and was running down the path. He'd fired a shot at me at the top. They, emphasizing the corporal and his men, should have heard it and seen the man running if they weren't asleep or drunk."

Letchworth looked at his men.

"Nobody came by us," Smyth whined.

"Like I said, you were either asleep or drunk or maybe you didn't want to see him," Cole responded. Smyth didn't comment to that.

Sergeant Duncannon walked up with a squad of men. "Captain, the boy's right. We could see a man running down the path but it was too far to see who it was."

The captain looked at Smyth. "We'll talk more about this later."

They all walked back up the path together, to the horses. The horses were still wet and lathered.

"Look at this, Captain," Sergeant Duncannon called.

Letchworth wiped a large spot on the saddle with his fingers and held it to the torch. "Blood! I have no idea how bad, but you hit the man." Letchworth told Cole.

"That's probably why he left the road," Cole replied. "Apollo was closing fast."

"Do any of you recognize the horse?" Letchworth asked. Nobody answered. "Sergeant, take the men back to the castle. I'll ride with Cole and see if we can find any evidence that will identify our man."

The musket was handed back to Cole, as they mounted their horses. "It's not mine," he said. "I picked it up where the shooter dropped it."

"It's too fine a gun for the likes of them, so you keep it," Letchworth said. "If the rogue wants it back, give it to him...barrel end first."

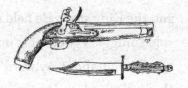

CHAPTER TWENTY NINE

P ADDY O'HARE SAT ON THE porch talking with Joe and Cole.

It was a week since the would-be assassin had taken a shot at Cole on that very porch. Joe had turned the corner in that week, and it looked like he might live. His appetite was back and he was able to get about better. He was still pale, though. Yet, in Joe lived the desire to find the man who had killed Peg, the riding officer, and nearly killed him. It had to be the same rogue who had shot at Cole.

"It was pure providence," Paddy was saying. "The last load had landed when the shot rang out. The batmen spread out ready to meet the duty men. It was then that several more shots were fired only they were shooting up the path, not toward us. I had the tubmen leg it to the cave. The boat pushed off and we stayed at the cave for an hour. We then felt the duty men were gone so in small groups we went home."

Paddy's discussion of the events that night in front of Cole made him wonder if he was now to be fully trusted or Paddy didn't know when to hold his tongue. I doubt he has loose lips, Cole decided.

Cole realized that he walked a fine line between the smugglers and the King's law. He held no animosity for those that bought and sold smuggled goods, his uncle being one of them. He was not sure how he felt about Aylward and his ilk. He'd heard Sir William say that it took a lot of money to finance an operation such as the one in Deal. He also thought Sir George Aylward was not by himself. Cole was sure that two or three partners existed, perhaps more. That was why Joe had gone to different places in London: to make sure that the investors got their share. He had no proof obviously, but in Cole's mind there was little doubt.

Sir William had also said the men were traitors to their country. He remembered his father saying that if taxes were cut, there'd not be enough profit in smuggling to make it worthwhile. The government would collect more by reducing the tax than they did now at such high tax rates. But who really profited. Aylward and his type...yes. But mostly the French, the enemy, that's who benefitted the most. They were the ones collecting the English gold for their goods. They'd likely use that same gold to buy arms and pay mercenaries to fight the British.

***

Cole, old chum,

Our First Lieutenant, Colin Atwater, has been given temporary command of the armed cutter, HMS Resolution. Her captain, an old tarpaulin, has a severe case of gout. It's said his toes are so swollen that they look like sausages. I'd think that would not do much for the appetite.

Atwater, being a man with impeccable taste and sound judgment, has chosen me to join him during this outing. While a cutter does not carry the weight a ship of the line or even a frigate does, she does carry fourteen 4 pounder guns and ten swivels. As I have proven to be very adept at gunnery and more that a fair hand in navigation and seamanship, I'm sure I was the only logical choice. That or the captain felt I'd be the least missed. I prefer to think it was the first and not the latter.

I have found a local maiden who is fair to look upon to spend time with when we are in port. She is so enamored with your brother, she only charges me four shillings instead of her usual price of a crown. I consider this a bargain as she also provides a meal and wine; a cheap wine to be sure.

The master's mate who is also going on this venture told me there's every probability that we may be assigned to the Customs House for a while. However, if as Captain Best believes, our time away on this little lark will be short-lived in the advent of war with France. I'm told if the war does occur I will likely retire a rich captain or dead. The latter aspect does not appeal.

In closing, I must say that I hope your relationship with the beautiful Anne is progressing. If she grows tired of you, let me know and I'll show her how a true blade treats the fairer sex.

Till next time, I remain your loving brother,

Phillip

Cole read and then reread Phillip's letter. He seemed in good spirits. Cole wished he was. He'd agreed to accompany Joe on another trip to London. Joe would be taking Mary this time and they'd go in a proper coach, Sir George's, and they'd stay at Sir

George's flat as before. Though it was only a flat, Mary was sure to be intrigued by its finery.

The weather was starting to get colder. Cole had woken up needing a blanket last evening. This morning Chloe had a shawl wrapped around her shoulders when she made it to the tavern. It was less than a month until the Christmas celebration started. He'd never been away from Belcastle during this time of year. There had always been plenty of food and festive activity. Cole wondered if Phillip would be there this year. He hadn't mentioned it in his letter. Did the smugglers operate in the winter, Cole wondered. Was there ever a pause in the free trade? Probably not, unless the weather dictated it, he thought.

The winds coming off the channel could be very cold in the winter. Smugglers knew the Customs people would be less likely to venture out, so maybe they did continue year round. Cole would listen to see if he heard anything to answer his question. He was hesitant to ask for some reason. Maybe he knew too much already. Hopefully, he'd never be called to give testimony in court. The thought made him shudder.

***

IT WAS NOVEMBER 13TH. It was Anne's mother, Mary's birthday. They were having a celebration that day at the Blue Post Inn. Kimberly was giving Mary a party. Cole had gone to Dan Thompson's shop and bought her a beautiful brooch. He'd saved his money and still had to ask his uncle for a crown in order to pay for it. Angus had waved away Cole's promise to pay him back.

The Inn was closed to regular customers at six o'clock p.m. Seeing Mary dressed in all her finery made Cole think of Linda. Did she have such outfits? Another thought came to Cole, since Eriksson had been gone for several months now, how was she managing? Did she have money to survive on? Cole made a mental note to find out.

The door opened allowing a gust of wind to enter. Cole turned to look and was surprised to see Andrea. She was without Sir George. Cole mentioned her arrival to Anne.

"Cole, there's very few women either Mother or Andrea have to associate with. While father and Sir George rarely speak, Mother and Andrea talk and visit often. They both take things to the orphanage and church, often together. Father fumes and I imagine so does Sir George. But that doesn't stop mother and Ms. Andrea from being friends. Of course, what father and Sir George do is never brought up."

Anne asked her mother's permission for her and Cole to walk down to the beach and back.

"Bundle up," Mary said, essentially giving her permission.

Kimberly met them at the door, "Don't be long. We'll serve dinner in about half an hour."

"We'll be back," Cole said.

A chilling blast hit them as they walked out the door. It was made worse after being in the heat of the inn. As they walked down toward Beach Street, they were passed by a group of Preventive Services men on horseback. One of them was Corporal Smyth, only his arm was now bare of his corporal's chevrons. Smyth glared at Cole, as they rode by, making a motion like slitting a throat.

"I shall tell father," Anne swore.

"No, I'll handle it when the time comes," Cole said. He then explained to Anne the circumstances causing the man's action.

They were near the tavern now. "Let's take a look at Apollo," Anne suggested.

Walking down the side of the tavern and into the stable, the smell of horses was strong. Just inside the door, Anne stopped, and tugged on Cole's arm. As he turned around, Anne locked her arms around his neck and the back of his head. After a long passionate kiss they broke apart.

"God, Anne, you are one woman who knows how to set a man on fire with desire."

"I'm on fire as well, Cole. I want you right here, right now. Take me if you want me," she said. Cole reached for Anne, pulling her to him again, crushing her breasts to his chest.

Errk...the sound of wood scrubbing on wood caused Cole and Anne to turn. It was Sidney. "I...I'm...sorry. I didn't know that anyone was in here."

"We were just looking at Apollo," Cole said.

"You might want to light the lantern for better light," the boy said, taking the lantern off its post.

"No, we have to be on our way," Cole said.

Sidney threw up his hand, "Bye."

"Damn," Cole hissed, once they were away from the stable.

This set Anne to laughing. "Better then, than when I had my dress up."

Cole was laughing now. "Or my pants down."

Anne laughed harder for a minute and then abruptly stopped. "Is it wrong for us to want, to desire each other so much, Cole?"

"No, I'd say that was normal, but society would frown on it and your father certainly would. In fact, I'm sure that he'd run me through with his blade."

"Oh Cole, I never thought of that. I just know I want you and I'm going to have you. I told mother and father if you got your commission and had to leave, I'd bed you married or not."

Cole stopped and pulled Anne to him, paying little regard to people passing them. "You know that I'd never do anything to hurt your name...your reputation. But I've promised myself, to ask your father for your hand at Christmas."

"Were you going to tell me?"

Cole smiled, "I just did."

They kissed, and then hand in hand, they walked back to the Blue Post Inn. Sir William was outside the entrance to the inn talking to Captain Letchworth.

Cole and Anne were close enough to hear Sir William tell Captain Letchworth, "If we get hard evidence on Frawley, I will bring him to trial."

Cole knew Frawley was one of Constable Oaks' men. Had he been caught taking money from the smugglers? Sir William wanted more proof than hearsay.

Sir William glanced their way and then back at Letchworth. He then turned back to Cole and Anne.

"We saw a squad of your men, Captain," Cole said. "Smyth didn't appear too happy with me." He threw this out to hopefully give Sir William the idea that they'd been in view of the public the entire time.

Letchworth smiled, "Yes, I took his corporal's stripe. His group admitted that they'd fallen asleep. Your shot scared the devil out of them. I'm glad you weren't injured when they shot back at you."

"They were shooting uphill and I ducked down behind a rock," Cole responded.

"Rodney tells me that you put a ball into the assassin," Sir William said. "Hopefully, he'll die from it. It's getting cold out here so I'll go back in. Rodney, you are welcome to join us."

"Thank you, Sir William, but I've other obligations."

Cole noted two things during that exchange. Sir William was without his coat so he must have already been inside. Did he know how long they'd been away? Also, by the use of the captain's first name, they were friends. It was not just a relationship between a captain and the magistrate. That might be worth remembering.

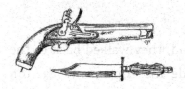

CHAPTER THIRTY

THE TRIP TO LONDON, THIS time, was more pleasant than the previous one. Sir George's coach was comfortable. The conversation was genial. Mary, Joe's fiancée, and Andrea, Sir George's wife, traveled well together. Andrea treated Mary more like a friend than an underling. Thinking about it, Anne's words came back to Cole, about there being very few women that Andrea or her mum could socialize with.

While Mary's father was a yeoman farmer, he'd done very well for himself. Cole had heard Joe mention that the Stuarts had a hops field which was used by brewers to make beer. This was a good cash crop. He also grew wheat, oats, and barley. The barley was also used for making beer. He also had a stand of apple and pear trees. John Stuart might not be as well off as Sir William or Sir George, but then again he might.

Some people didn't seem to need a lot. Was John Stuart one of these? Mary certainly seemed to dress well. Was this due to Deal's cheap prices or because they had money. After a bit of reflection, Cole bet that they had money. That was why Joe worked as he did, so that Mary would have the same standard of living.

When they reached the coach inn, where they were spending the night, Cole got a chance to speak to Joe about Linda.

"She told me, Joe that Leif provided for her. Since he's been missing, I wonder who makes sure that she's taken care of."

"Good question," Joe responded. "I know that John and Mary share out of their garden."

"But there's other things that she needs," Cole said.

"I'll write a note and leave it here for Paddy, to speak to Sir George about it. He should be on the return trip now. He's been delivering supplies."

"Thanks, Joe, I appreciate it."

Joe waved Cole's remarks away. "The way I see it, Sir George owes you a favor, a few actually."

The trip to London was extended an extra day and a half due to the weather. It stormed the night before the morning they were to leave. Howling winds roared over the houses and streets of London. Volleys of rain slammed into the glass windows, and drops coming down the chimney caused the fire to hiss and spit. When morning came, the darkness made one think it was still night. Black clouds scudded across the sky visible with flashes of lightning. Thunder would start to rumble way off, growing louder as it got near, and then boom. The china would shake in the cabinet, at times.

"I'm glad that we finished our errands when we did," Mary said.

"Yes," Andrea agreed. "I'm glad I'm not out on the water now."

She was talking about crossing the channel to Calais, which would be dangerous in such weather. It made Cole think of Phillip on the cutter. He'd not answered his letter yet, so now would be a good time, he decided.

***

THE WOMEN WERE WISHING THEY'D lain over one more day by the time they got back to Deal. The roads had eroded and the potholes were more frequent and deep. However, after reaching the coaching inn, the remainder of the road to Deal was much better. By the time Cole was back at the tavern, he had lost some of the soreness he'd gotten riding the first half of the trip back from London in the bouncing coach. Once the coach bounced so hard Andrea almost landed on the floor, Cole reached out to catch her. As he grabbed Andrea, his hands and arms encircled her chest and he felt her ample breasts. Embarrassed, he apologized.

"Nonsense," Andrea said. "Better that than bruising my backside."

Joe grabbed at his wound. "Damn that driver," he said, and leaned out the window and told the driver to slow down or taste his blade.

Cole laughed, "Taste your blade, Joe?"

The thought made the women laugh as well. Finally, Joe smiled.

His uncle waved as he entered but continued talking with a customer. Aunt Florence gave him a hug and said that she was glad to see he was home. Sidney saw him and rushed over, placing an arm across his shoulder.

"You've a letter on your pillow," Sidney said.

"From who?" Cole asked.

"A lady I'd say."

"From Anne," Cole guessed.

"No, I think it is from that other lady."

Cole rushed to his room and tore open the letter. It was more a note, but it spoke volumes.

Dearest Cole,

Paddy O'Hare was by today dropping off a purse filled with gold coin. He said it was a portion of what was owed to you. He further said that you were very concerned about my welfare, more so because of this assassin

running about. How can I thank you. Of course, we both know how I could try but I'm sure that was not the expectation. I feel you love me and I do love you. If only it was another place in time...If.

I saw you with Anne, and you look the perfect pair. I think I could be friends with your future wife.

Please be careful. I will worry as I think of you racing through the night on your steed chasing assassins.

I remain your dearest and most loyal friend.

The note was not signed but it didn't need to be, Cole thought. Anybody but a fool would know whom it was from. A purse full of gold coin. Sir George had done well, Cole thought. I guess that puts us even. What will he want next, Cole then wondered. Did the man do anything without expecting something in return. If he did expect something, Cole decided, it would only happen if he so chose to do it.

Thinking of the wedding ring that Joe had gotten Mary, Cole thought maybe something would come up. He needed to earn some money so that he could buy Anne a ring. It was not that long until Christmas.

***

COLE WAS NOW GETTING USED to the road to Canterbury. Joe had come to him the Saturday after the trip to London. If Cole was up to it, he could drive a wagon and unload merchandise in Sandwich and Canterbury. His uncle had not objected, though both of them knew he would be hauling contraband. Cole had told Anne he was going home for a couple of days. He wanted to inform his parents that he was going to ask for her hand in marriage. He also wanted to hear the latest on his commission. A year had not passed so he didn't want to be a nuisance, but he didn't want any last minute surprises either. The talk lately at the tavern was more and more about the upcoming war. Cole couldn't help but wonder how him being away would affect Anne. She'd, at least, have her parents close at hand.

A run had been made while Cole and Joe had been in London. The lugger's captain had left word saying, 'Dunkirk was full of French soldiers.'

"Think the war will have any effect on supplies?" Cole asked. He had learned to use that term rather than smuggling.

"It never has, it usually gets easier. Our biggest problem is keeping our men out of the press gang's hands," Joe said.

"You don't have a signal or something set up for that?" Cole asked.

Shaking his head no, Joe said, "It's like a verse in the bible, 'They come like a thief in the night.'"

CHAPTER THIRTY ONE

IT WAS A WEEK UNTIL the beginning of Christmas celebration. Mary, Anne's mother, and other ladies were gathering items to make garlands and things to decorate the church and take to the orphanage. There already was talk about the planned festivities. Around Deal, shops were filled with all sorts of foods and the bakery was busy preparing sweet breads, pastries, and pies.

While Joe and Cole made their trip to Canterbury, the smugglers had made another run. This one had proven to be ill-fated. When the tubmen were given their last loads, a Customs cutter fired on the smugglers' ship. Duty men then tried to surround the smugglers on land. The batmen and tubmen, fearing prison or worse, fired on the duty men. From the shore to the wagons at the top of the cliffs, orange flames from the muzzles of muskets and pistols flashed in the night. The sound of gunfire was so great that people in Deal broke with tradition and looked out doors and windows.

Once the weapons were fired, it became hand-to-hand combat, blade and club. It looked like the duty men would prevail for a bit, but the sheer number of the determined smugglers kept pressing against the duty men. Paddy O'Hare found himself fighting three of the duty men at one time. A duty man lunged at Paddy with his blade at one point, and Paddy dodged the blade and spun the man so that a charging duty man was impaled by his comrade's sword. Paddy laid the other two out with his club. When the fight was over, Sergeant Duncannon and a squad went out looking for those duty men that were missing.

When they were found, it was discovered that it was Smyth who was dead by a fellow duty man's blade. Neither of the two surviving men could identify who they were fighting or how Smyth came to be killed. Other than Smyth, there were no other deaths, though some on both sides were seriously injured.

The lugger captain was able to slip away while the cutter was grounded on the Goodwin Sands. Cole learned from Sir William that an informer had sent a note to Captain Letchworth about the landing. With the smugglers winning the night, Letchworth swore he'd call out the army the next time.

"There likely won't be a next time for a while, not with the Christmas celebration being near," Joe mused.

Cole hoped not, but if so, he hoped that Joe wouldn't be involved. The Customs people seemed to be getting more aggressive.

***

COLE HAD FINALLY RECEIVED AN allowance that had been accumulating from his father. He waited until he had his mother, father, and the Earl together to announce his plans to ask Sir William for Anne's hand.

"She is so young," his mother said.

"And I may not get much older, Mother." Cole's reply startled everyone. "If the war starts as predicted and my unit is called into battle, I may not get much older. So you see, time is precious to Anne and me."

The attitude at the table changed. At first, they were stunned that such a possibility existed, that in war Cole and Phillip could fall at any time. Peter put his arm around his wife.

"A toast to Cole," the Earl said. "May his marriage be a long and prosperous one, with sons and daughters a plenty."

After dinner that evening, the Earl had Cole follow him to his office. He took a key from his desk and walked to the bookshelf. He pushed on a shelf and the entire panel turned, revealing an iron door. Opening the door, the Earl pulled out a tray of jewels. Looking about, he pulled out a beautiful emerald ring.

"This was my grandmother's," he said. "I want you to have it for your lady."

"I don't know what to say," Cole began.

"Say nothing. It's done nothing but collect dust for years."

Cole couldn't remember the last time he'd actually hugged Charles Bickford, Earl of Belcastle, but he did so then and was embraced back.

"You and Phillip have no idea what joy you've given an old man. I've come to realize, with you both being gone, just how much the two of you kept your father and me going."

The Earl now held Cole at arm's length so that he could look the boy in the eye. "You know your father is my most trusted friend. Your mother has raised Catherine and Phillip as her own. You are a part of Belcastle. When I die, I've set aside a thousand acres to be yours. I know that you and Phillip plan on raising horses together, so the two of you may choose to never divide the holdings. But should you decide to, yours has been written down. Also, when I pass, Phillip will become Earl of Belcastle. But should he be killed, Belcastle will be yours in its entirety. Should you fall, your holdings will be Phillip's. I trust you both to do right by Catherine and each of your families, should there be any."

The Earl placed the tray of jewels back and locked the door, then turned the shelf back around. "I had this talk with Phillip at your birthday celebration. He understands completely. One more thing, Cole, your father and mother will remain at Belcastle as long as they live. I wanted you to know that, to be assured by me. You've never questioned it, but now you know."

"Thank you, sir," was all that Cole could think to say.

Back at Deal now, Cole planned a dinner for Anne and her parents at Kimberly Jordan's Inn. She had said, "Leave it to me," when Cole had approached her.

His Uncle Angus had declined the invitation, saying this needs to be a small, private affair. "I'd like as not strangle Sir William if he doesn't consent."

The meal was a huge success. Good wine to match each entrée and then a dessert that almost made Cole forget why they were there. In fact, he'd just sat back in his chair to get comfortable and digest his meal when Anne jabbed him. He smiled at Anne, holding her hand beneath the table. He looked at Mary and she was also smiling. Did she know or guess what the occasion for this meal was?

Drawing himself up straight and taking a breath, Cole said, "Sir William, Lady Brabham, I don't think there's any secret about how I feel about your daughter or how she feels about me. Therefore, we would like to get married, but before I ask for her hand, you should know I will be able to provide for her. You both know that I'm to be commissioned. A letter that was waiting for me at home said to expect to be called in late February or March. While in the army, I'm to have an allowance of one hundred guineas a year. When I reach twenty-one, or sooner should the Earl die, heaven forbid, I shall have one thousand acres. Should Phillip fall, Belcastle will be mine." Both of Anne's parents seemed to be holding their breath. "I felt it was important that you know that I can provide for Anne in a manner in which she has been accustomed. I hope having set your mind at ease as to my being able to provide for Anne, you will respond favorably to my question." Cole paused and then spoke again, "I now ask for the honour of marrying your daughter."

Cole was not sure what Sir William had planned to say or would have said, but Mary was smiling and clapping her hands, her consent essentially given.

"Cole, there's times I've doubted decisions you've made," Sir William said. "But I've never doubted your honesty or your love for my daughter. I think she fell in love with you in front of Angus's tavern the day you met."

"Oh, I did, Father," Anne responded.

"Have you thought of a date?" Mary asked.

Anne answered quickly, "Tomorrow if it were possible, but in truth, before Cole has to join his regiment."

"There's one thing," Cole said, "and should you decide against it, I will understand. This is Anne's home. However, the Earl would like to have the wedding at Belcastle, if possible."

Sir William responded quickly, "I leave that up to the women. Being the magistrate hasn't made me the most popular person in Deal, so the ones that I'd invite can just as easily go to Belcastle, I'm sure."

Anne laughed and Lady Brabham cried. They hugged each other and then Anne got up and walked around to her father.

"Thank you so much, Father. I love you so much."

Cole kissed Mary and then shook Sir William's hand, thanking him. Kimberly stuck her head in, just as Anne kissed Cole. She smiled and thought, things have gone well.

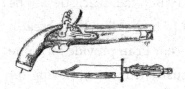

CHAPTER THIRTY TWO

T HE APPEARANCE OF AN ARMED cutter off the beach of Deal had rumors flying and some making their way inland for fear of the press gangs. Those who didn't fear the press gangs went down to the beach as a boat put off from the cutter.

Dalton, who had been headed to the beach, stopped at the tavern. Sticking his head in the entrance, he saw Cole stocking boxes filled with freshly rolled cigars. "A boat from a cutter is coming ashore, Cole."

Those at the tavern had heard about the cutter, like everybody else. Chloe, with a shawl on her shoulders and barefoot, went down to see the excitement along with Cole and Dalton.

Dalton gently tapped Cole on the shoulder. "I can't see how you don't go blind. Chloe is a beautiful piece of mutton if I ever saw one. Other than Anne, she's the prettiest girl in Deal."

"Ask her out for dinner," Cole suggested.

"Father would disown me if I did. He wants a title in the family, so I'm to marry into it or gain a knighthood in battle. He's got all the money a person could want. Now he's after recognition."

Cole understood, he'd seen it before–landed people with money marrying someone with a title, especially if the peerage individual was broke.

The crowd watched as the boat made its way in, the bow grinding into the wet sand. A sailor jumped out and pulled the boat further up onto the beach. Cole quickly recognized the one in a blue uniform. "Mr. Midshipman Phillip Bickford is that you?" he called.

The midshipman turned, "Cole! It is a good day. I had hoped that I'd see you."

"Are you free or do you need to stay by the boat?" Cole asked.

"I've been sent ashore to arrange transportation for our captain to go to Deal Castle," Phillip said.

"It's not far but if he'd like to ride, I will loan him Apollo."

"I'd say, old chap," Phillip replied, putting on airs, "that would be just grand."

Phillip turned to a man standing by the boat. "Browne, go back to the cutter and inform the captain that my own brother is here and is willing to loan him his horse. A most magnificent steed he is too, Browne."

"Aye," the man said as he climbed back into the boat and they pushed off.

"How far is it?" Phillip asked.

"Just up the hill. We have a couple of other horses if you need to accompany your captain."

"Thanks, we'll see what his honour wishes," Phillip replied.

Cole then realized that he'd been remiss and hadn't introduced Dalton. After introductions, Phillip said, "Who is that goddess walking toward us?"

Cole smiled. Dalton wasn't the only one to notice the girl's beauty. Come to think of it, Cole thought, out on the beach like this, with the breeze blowing Chloe does look beautiful. Why did it take others to make me appreciate her beauty?

"Chloe," Cole called. "I want you to meet my brother, Phillip Bickford. Phillip, this is Chloe."

Phillip gave an exaggerated bow and then kissed the back of Chloe's hand. "It is indeed a pleasure to meet such an angelic lady such as yourself. I hardly know your name, my dear, and I'm hopelessly in love."

The girl smiled, "And you, kind sir, are as full of blarney as your Uncle Angus."

"I don't dispute your words, dear lady, but in your case it's true."

The boat carrying Lieutenant Colin Atwater, acting captain of the cutter, landed ashore about the time Cole and Phillip got Apollo and another horse saddled and made it back down to the beach, where the boat landed. Dalton had taken his leave while Chloe seemed to be floating on clouds back at the tavern.

"Captain Atwater," Phillip said, using Atwater's title rather than rank. "I'd like to introduce you to my older brother. He was too dumb to be a midshipman so he's being commissioned in the Army."

Atwater proved to be a jovial sort. "He probably has more going for him than either of us," Atwater replied. He then took in Apollo. "That's the most beautiful horse I've ever seen," he exclaimed. "Damned if it isn't."

This made Cole swell with pride. "Thank you, sir. Deal Castle is just down this road. A sign marks it but it's visible long before you get there," Cole said.

"Would you like for me to accompany you, sir?" Phillip asked.

"I think not, Mr. Bickford. I shall call on you when I return."

"Just ask for the Cock and Bull, sir," Cole said. "If time permits, I'd like for you to join us for an early dinner."

"If time permits," Atwater agreed.

IT WAS GETTING CLOSE TO dusk before Atwater returned from his meeting with Captain Letchworth. Walking into the Cock and Bull he paused, taking in the assortment of cigars available. After a quick look he walked into the taproom. Phillip and Cole rose from their table to meet him.

Chloe was over quickly to take Atwater's drink request. Like Phillip, he couldn't take his eyes off the girl.

After getting a glass of wine, Atwater spoke, "Captain Letchworth states that you could direct me to Sir William Brabham's house."

"Yes, sir, seeing as I'm to wed his daughter."

"Congratulations, sir. I have need to speak with him tomorrow morning if that can be arranged."

"I'm sure it can, sir. I could ride out now."

"That would be good. I will go back to the cutter. Take Mr. Bickford with you. He can return and let me know the plans once you've spoken to Sir William. Make a signal, Phillip, and I'll send a boat to pick you up."

After Atwater had picked out a handful of cigars, which Angus gave to him, he left. While Phillip was speaking to Chloe, Angus spoke to Cole.

"I don't like the idea of them bringing in a naval cutter to be helping with the Customs people. It's sure to cause a lot of trouble. Some of the blokes are sure to get hurt, killed, or in prison before this is over."

"Not if they don't have any landings," Cole said.

"Aye, but that 'if' is a big word, lad."

The ride to Sir William's house was taken up with talk of Cole and Anne's wedding, especially how surprised Cole had been at how easily Sir William had said yes to holding the wedding at Belcastle.

Phillip said, after a bit, "You are a better man than I, Cole. I can't believe with Chloe around that you haven't topped the girl. I'm sure Anne causes your humours to run wild."

"In truth, until today I hadn't really noticed the girl," Cole replied.

"You are either blind or someone else was putting out the fire," Phillip responded.

"Aye," Cole agreed with a pang of guilt. But they were now at the Brabham's so he didn't have to explain further.

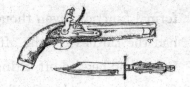

CHAPTER THIRTY THREE

THE WEDDING WAS SET FOR January 1st. What better way to start the new year than as man and wife. On the 24th of December, Cole with Anne, her parents, and Kimberly Jackson rode to Canterbury. Cole's mother had been in communication frequently since he'd sent word that Anne and her family agreed to have the wedding at Belcastle.

Joe and Mary were going to ride over on New Year's morning with Sir George and Andrea. Cole joked with Anne about having Sir George and her father under the same roof.

She laughed and said, "It's good that the ceremony is being held at Belcastle. They will both have to be on their best behavior."

Phillip had requested time off so that he could be home for Christmas and the wedding. Atwater was being hosted by Captain Letchworth at Deal Castle for the holidays. Uncle Angus and Aunt Florence would have Christmas at the tavern and come over the day before the wedding.

Joe had been very hesitant, even nervous about attending a formal function, even though Sir George had made sure that he had the clothes for the affair. Dalton had been invited but his father had begged off, citing previous obligations. The more Cole found out about Mr. Stephenson, the less he cared about him. If people thought Sir George seemed to have an abundance of money, they didn't know Mr. Dwight Stephenson very well. He had more people working for him in some capacity other than a laborer than Sir George; far more if you just looked at the amount of time they spent at the tavern and the number of cigars they bought. Dalton had said that his father had holdings from Scotland to London and more. Where did the man make such money? If Dalton was to be believed, his father always had beautiful women over.

Cole could only remember speaking to the man once. He had said to Cole, "You boy, come here if you will." Cole had told him his name but the man waved it off as if it were of no consequence. He'd bought two boxes of Angus' best cigars. Cole had not seen the man since. Of course, some of his men might have been buying cigars for him.

Dalton rarely spoke positively of his father other than to say he planned on buying a peerage. Joe had once told Cole that Dalton was neglected. He could see that now and was glad that he had offered the hand of friendship to Dalton.

***

ANNE AND COLE RODE THEIR horses while her parents and Kimberly rode in the family carriage with Henry driving. At the halfway point, they drew up to give the horses a breather. It had not rained in several days and the Canterbury road was very dry and dusty.

Cole was glad that he'd let Dan Thompson wrap up the presents he'd bought his mother and Catherine. Otherwise they'd have to be washed before they could be worn; silk shawls and dust were no match. He'd also bought Anne's mother one and, unbeknownst to anyone other than Dan, he had sent one to Linda also. The card had simply said, 'From a dear friend.' She would know whom it was from.

It had stunned him when Anne had mentioned her feelings on inviting Linda to the wedding. He didn't know what to say, but Anne had started laughing.

"I was only joking," she said.

Cole breathed a sigh of relief. That had been an awkward moment. While the two of them, Linda and he, had each made a vow to themselves not to resume their lovemaking, you just didn't turn off the friendship. It would be out of necessity a distant friendship, but nevertheless a friendship.

The group made Canterbury in the late afternoon. The church had been decorated for Christmas. Cole was amazed that the archbishop had agreed to perform the wedding ceremony on such short notice. However, with the war looming and the Earl's influence, and no doubt a sizeable contribution, an agreement was made.

＊

COLE BUCKLEY STOOD IN THE great room at Belcastle, with his bride at his side. The archbishop was speaking, but Cole was thinking, we stand before God, our family and friends and I vow there'll never be anyone else but you, my sweet Anne. She squeezed his hand, breaking his reverie.

"I do," Cole said, not sure if that was what was being asked, but was relieved when the archbishop continued.

The ceremony was over then, and they were man and wife. The reception proved to be, what seemed to Cole, a neverending line of well wishers.

Catherine had whispered in his ear, "You rogue, you beat me to the honeymoon chamber." She then said, "Samuel has proposed. He will ask for father's permission soon."

Cole thought, I'll be going to war with Major Samuel Huntington as my brother-in-law. The major had just kissed Anne's hand.

He then faced Cole, and said with a wink, "Who'd have thought this would take place when we met at the tavern, Cole. I know that Catherine has told you I've proposed to her. I will depend on you to fill me in on all I need to know."

Cole had always thought of Catherine as a sister. But like he'd seen Chloe differently when Phillip had brought his attention to the girl, he now saw Catherine in a different light. She was a beautiful woman, all right, and a most beautiful woman. He suddenly felt sad that he'd never really paid attention to the painting of her mother that hung in the Earl's office. He was glad his mother had been there for Catherine. Another thought came to Cole. She must have been some woman indeed for the Earl to have never taken another wife. His father had said once, 'For some men there can be but one.'

Cole realized, looking back, that the Earl had a mistress here and there but that was it. Was it because if he'd married, Cole's mother, the substitute mother of his children, would no longer be the mistress of Belcastle? Or was it that the Earl had not found a woman he felt would take the place of his wife as his father had hinted. If so, that was a strong love. Cole wondered if his love for Anne matched that. Would he, if circumstances changed, be able to resume his relationship with the widow? He thought not.

The reception was over. All of their friends and relatives had been greeted, and presents were given. They'd eaten a feast and then danced it off. They were now going to another part of Belcastle. One that he and Phillip had once ventured into years ago. It was set up as a separate suite and contained a master bedroom, huge closet, and an area with a commode and bathtub. There were also rooms for children. Cole and Phillip had never been back and it had never been used. Had it been for the Earl before he was the Earl?

"Following the maid servant?" Anne asked. "What did Phillip say to you as we left?"

Cole smiled, "He said, 'she got you today, tonight you'll get her.' He was most envious." Anne smiled. "Did you think Joe looked the part of a gentleman?" Cole asked.

"Yes," Anne smiled. "An uncomfortable one."

"I keep thinking of him bashing heads in the ring, and not ever thinking he'd look so gentlemanly dressed up." Cole added.

"He could dance, as well," Anne volunteered.

Cole started to respond but the maid had stopped.

The maid opened the door to their suite and Anne was amazed. It was almost an apartment.

"They've just drawn warm water and the tub is ready, should you care for a bath," the maid said with a wink at Anne.

Once the door was closed, Anne looked at Cole, "I've waited so long for this night. I've dreamed of it since we first met, and now I'm nervous that I'll be a disappointment."

"Never," Cole said as they kissed.

The kiss was long and passionate, creating a frenzy. He had to help unlace the back of Anne's gown. If he had a knife, he'd have slit the damn laces. Finally, they were there alone, no clothes on, facing one another, taking in each other's bodies.

Anne's breasts, her beautiful breasts, would rise with every breath. Cole kissed her mouth, her eyes and neck, and when he reached her breast, Anne gave out a tiny cry as his mouth found her hard nipple. He picked her up and carried her to the bed. They kissed again, creating a raging fire of passion.

"Oh God, Cole, now. Let me feel you now."

The first round of lovemaking was hurried as each hungered for the other. A burning flame that could only be quenched one way. Anne's fingers clawed into Cole's back, as their lovemaking reached a crescendo until they both exploded. Spent from their passion, they fell back exhausted but not through.

"I hope I didn't hurt you," Cole said.

"You could have split me open and I wouldn't have cared," Anne said. "I wanted you, all of you inside me. I didn't know anything could feel so good, so special," she added, nuzzling Cole's neck as he held her close. She then rose up, with her beautiful breasts right before his eyes. "I didn't disappoint you, did I, Cole?"

Seeing his wife there, her little nose slightly upturned, her full lips and those firm, ripe breasts only inches away from his eyes and mouth. He asked, "How could you? I was in heaven." He pulled her on top of him then and took her breast in his mouth again. Anne moved to give him better access to each breast, as he devoured one and then the other.

This time their lovemaking was slow and deliberate as each explored the other's body. Touching, feeling, and kissing until their passion exploded.

Sometime later as they went to the tub, Anne said, "It's just tepid."

"We can warm it up," Cole replied.

Anne looked at her new husband. "Do you not grow tired?"

Cole smiled at her, "You bring life into me each time I think of your beautiful body."

"Come heat up the water then, dear husband. Your wife awaits you."

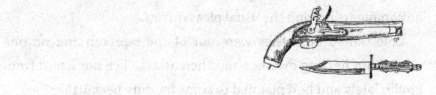

CHAPTER THIRTY FOUR

EAL WAS COLD, AND THE wind traveled up Broad Street causing a body to pull his cloak closer. White caps crashed ashore off the channel. Cole and his new bride had returned to Deal after a week in Canterbury and Belcastle. Anne and Catherine had become friends. The two of them, along with Cole's mother, Margaret, discussed Catherine's upcoming wedding.

Cole had promised Angus that he'd watch the tavern while he and Aunt Florence went to London. It was conceivably the last time that he'd be able to watch the tavern before reporting for his commission.

Major Huntington had received word to report February 1st. Cole expected to receive word soon after that.

For a day so cool it seemed like a lot of people were out. Joe had dropped by and said there was talk of a landing that night; not theirs but someone's.

"It's going to be a hell of a job to haul in supplies, as cold as it is," Joe said. "I'm glad that it's not us."

Captain Letchworth stopped in for a handful of cigars but made no comments beyond the usual pleasantries.

Cole waited until they were out of the taproom and no one was within hearing distance and then asked, "I've not heard from Phillip lately and he'd planned to come by, duty permitting."

Captain Letchworth eyed Cole for several moments before he spoke. "I guess the key, Cole, is duty permitting." He then leaned in close to Cole. "Last I was told, they are assisting the Preventive Agents in Hastings." Cole nodded but didn't speak.

Joe and Paddy stopped by just before closing that night. Joe said, "Alfred Square is full of drunken louts. If I was in charge of this landing, I'd wave it off, if I was able."

"Aye," Paddy agreed. "I told two of our lads not to be consorting with the likes of them."

It was after midnight when a gang of men passed the tavern, some of them still drinking and singing. Anne went to look out the window but Cole pulled her back.

"Those that see nothing, can't be asked anything," he said.

Anne looked puzzled. Cole tried to explain the situation to her. The sound of a bottle or jug crashing in the street reached them.

"That's not the usual way smugglers act," he said. He then added, "This night has failure written all over it, damned if it don't."

"Failure?" Anne asked. "How do you know?"

"I know enough to know if you're pulling off some illegal activity, you don't march through the street waking the town without worrying about the constables being alerted."

"What do we do?" Anne asked. "Just sit here and do nothing."

"I can think of something to do," Cole answered with a smile, and twitching his eyebrows.

Anne smiled, "What's keeping you?"

***

COLE AWOKE SUDDENLY, AND ROSE up. Anne was also roused. There it was again, a gunshot. Voices were audible in the street. Shouts, curses and another shot followed by a cry of pain. A look of fear came over Anne, as the voices grew louder and came nearer to the tavern.

"That was father's voice. Father is down there." Saying that, Anne bounded to the window.

Cole pulled her back, "You've no clothes on, woman."

"I don't care, Cole that was father."

Cole had pulled on his britches and stomped his feet into his boots. He grabbed his two pistols, making sure that they were primed and loaded.

"Lock this door when I go out," he instructed Anne. "And stay away from the window."

Once on the street, the shouts were coming just to the north of him. He heard and then saw Anne's father with a pistol in hand and the constable next to him. One of the constable's men was down with a growing puddle of dark blood oozing from under him.

"Sir William," Cole called, wishing to identify himself so that he wouldn't get shot at. He ran over to where the two men were.

Sir William reached over and took a white armband off the downed constable. "Put this on, Cole."

"Yes sir," Cole replied.

The constable raised his head to see if the smugglers were still there. A pistol shot rang out and the ball thudded into the wall of the bakery.

"Letchworth is taking his men around and coming up from the rear," Sir William explained. "We are trying to keep them from running back toward the beach."

Cole nodded and reached out, taking a pistol from the dead man.

The shrill sound of a whistle broke the temporary silence. After the whistle came the sound of charging men. There were more shouts and gunshots, followed by curses. The duty men were doing their job. A mass of men rushed the intersection where Cole, Sir William, and the constable were hiding.

"Halt! In the King's name, halt," the constable shouted.

This did not stop or even slow the mob down. There were more shots fired in the direction of Cole's group. All three men returned fire.

"Damme," Sir William swore as a ball burned his arm.

Cole fired a shot and saw a man fall; and then he shot at a man training a musket on them. Cole had the satisfaction of seeing that villain fall as well.

Captain Letchworth was now upon them with his men. Some of the gang continued running on down to the beach. Some of them even went into the water hoping to escape.

By the time dawn arrived, eight bodies were found dead. This included one of the duty men and the constable's man, Frawley. Whether or not he had been in the smuggler's pay, it mattered little now. They had captured eleven of the smugglers. The local gaol was too small, so most of the men were chained together and then to a tree near the gaol.

"A good evening's work," the constable said.

"The dregs," Sir William said. "A rowdy lot, most of whom were drunk before the night even started. Someone supplied the drink to get these men drunk. I doubt that half of them even know what they are locked up for."

Sir William looked at Captain Letchworth and the constable. "We will have court starting at 8:00 tomorrow morning. Now I'm going home to a bath and to bed."

"I'd take it kindly, Sir William, if you'd stop by and speak to Anne. She heard your voice last night, so I know she's worried sick," Cole said.

Sir William placed a hand on Cole's shoulder. "Quite right, me boy. I mustn't let her worry."

Anne was dressed and drinking cocoa when they arrived. "Oh God, I'm glad to see you both," she cried. "I had feared the worst with all the shooting."

"Poor shots, every one of them," Sir William exclaimed. "I was glad when Cole showed up, nevertheless. Without him, things may have been far worse."

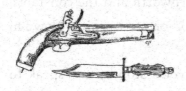

CHAPTER THIRTY FIVE

HE COURT APPEARANCE FOR THE smugglers was almost laughable. Five of those who were drunk when captured had no recollection of the night's events beyond being told there were free drinks at the Red Lion. It was a tavern noted for cheap women and cheaper spirits.

They didn't remember leaving the tavern, and when they woke up in chains, they were as amazed as anyone could be. Sir William believed them so he let them go with a warning about public drunkenness. Two more of the rogues were given one year prison terms in Newgate, and two more were sentenced to three years at Newgate, while two of the men who were known to have fired on the duty men or Sir William were sentenced to hang. One of them was wounded. Cole was sure that he was the one who shot the rogue, when he fired at Sir William, the constable, and himself.

Since the sentence of hanging could only be carried out officially by the Assize Court, the sentence was not official for the two smugglers. The Assize Court was only convened twice a year so those two men were sent to Newgate to await trial. However, it was widely understood that once a death sentence was given by the magistrate, the likelihood of it being changed was remote.

It was only later, when talking to Dalton, that Cole found out the men who had received the death sentences, which meant hanging, were in fact two of his father's men. Had they gotten involved in this smuggling on their own or were they just front men for Stephenson, not unlike what Eriksson had been for Sir George?

While walking and talking to Dalton, Cole couldn't help but bring up how obvious the group had been, going about the operation in such a loud, boastful, and drunken manner.

"Aye," Dalton said. "My father thinks someone supplied the alcohol to make sure it got out of control. He thinks the landing was set up for failure on purpose."

"I have to agree," Cole said. "I've known things to have happened, such as a landing going wrong, but never have I been awakened by such drunken idiots in the middle of the night."

Dalton never came right out and said that his father was involved in the smuggling operation, but by some of the comments he made, it caused Cole to wonder.

Joe came by the tavern later that day. The taproom was just starting to get crowded, but Chloe and Betsy were handling it well. With Angus gone to London, Agnes had come by to help out in the kitchen. Cole was about to tell her to wash her hands when he realized the brown on her fingers was from rolling cigars. He'd let her son, Jacob, help in the scullery since Sidney was with Angus and Florence. The money would certainly help and the two could eat at the tavern.

Cole was sorting the cigars Agnes had brought that day, with Joe at his side. "Have you ever seen or heard of such a mess with smugglers, Joe?"

Joe remained silent for a moment and then asked, "Are we talking between us and no one else?"

This shocked Cole but he knew his marrying the magistrate's daughter had caused the question. "It's between two friends, same as always, Joe."

Joe nodded and said, "Nothing about what's happened lately makes sense, Cole. Starting with Peg's murder, and somehow it's hard for me to see Leif shooting at someone from a hideout. I've seen him call out too many people to think he'd ambush a person. He lost a hefty purse on the fight and I'm sure his thoughts toward Linda were far from brotherly. Still, it doesn't all fit. He'd kill a man sure enough and if things had got out of hand with Peg...if she threatened him with the law, he'd kill. But something is dark about killings. Something dark indeed,"

"What about Sir George? Think he set things up the other night?" Cole asked.

Joe was blunt, "No, there's no profit in it. What happens should he need help? He can't go to a man who's suspicious that you got his men drunk or called the duty men on them. No, I'd wager Sir George had nothing to do with it. Also, the word is out since the Navy took a lugger in Hastings the other night. If Sir George had been involved, it would have been very quietly done. There'd have been no drinking or raising hell. I expect things to slow down anyway. Until the war pulls the Navy away, they'll be fewer landings as the risk will be greater. The Navy will sail a cutter across a heavy dew and fight her at the same time. The Customs captains are not so daring or trusting in their crew. Anyone of which might be on someone else's pay."

Cole nodded, "I heard my brother was involved at Hastings."

Joe replied, "We were told the same thing. There's some who are wondering if you can still be trusted."

Cole didn't ask who 'some' were. "I'll not stand by and see Phillip put into danger. Other than that, you have no need to worry about me, Joe."

"I know, Cole, but I'm not everyone. I will tell you; word is out that you shot Martin."

Who is Martin, Cole thought and then it came to him. "I'll shoot any man pointing a weapon at me. Others ran by and made it. He could have done the same; instead he chose to shoot at me."

Joe nodded his head and said, "I'll pass that along."

Cole smiled, "I had a pair of pistols that shoot true."

"Aye," Joe responded. "I'm glad that they came in handy...again."

"How's things with Mary?" Cole asked, recognizing that Joe was ready to leave.

"She's well and said thank you for inviting us to your wedding. We've never been in a castle before."

Cole said, "It's not a castle, it's a manor house."

Joe smiled, "Our room was bigger than my entire house."

"Be careful her father doesn't hear 'our room'," Cole replied smiling.

"You're a good friend, Cole." Without another word, the big man was gone.

Chloe came over later that night, as they were closing up the tavern. "This has your name on it, Cole."

Opening the envelope, Cole felt his heart skip a beat. 'Sir William is going to die. Stay away or your wife may join him'.

"Chloe," Cole called. "Who gave this to you?"

"No one, sir. I found it on a table. It wasn't there one minute, and then it was."

Cole was angry. He went to the stable and saddled Apollo. Anne was at her parents' house and Cole was glad of that. Once out of the stable yard, he let the stallion have its head. The house was dark except for a lamp in Anne's room and one in her parents' room. The doors to the house were never locked. Cole went in after tying Apollo to a post. He went to Sir William and Mary's bedroom.

Tapping on the door, it was a moment before Sir William answered, "Yes!"

"I've need to speak to you, sir."

Opening the door, Sir William found himself alarmed. Having never seen Cole in such a state, Sir William followed Cole down the hall and into his office. Lighting a candle, Cole took the note and handed it to his father-in-law. A frown creased Sir William's face.

Cole said, "I have no idea who left it. Chloe found it on a table and brought it to me."

"I've had my share of death threats," Sir William admitted, "but never once has my wife or child been included."

"They tell me to stay away," Cole said. "Away from what...away from whom?"

Sir William nodded. "From me, I'd say. Had you not been there, Martin may have shot me."

Cole asked, "Do you think that we should send Anne and Mary to Canterbury?"

Sir William thought a minute and then replied, "Mary would never go and I doubt Anne would either."

"We must be ever vigilant then sir," Cole said. "I shall go armed from now on."

Sir William nodded, "I shall also."

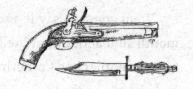

CHAPTER THIRTY SIX

PHILLIP WAS HAVING DINNER WITH Cole and Anne at the Blue Post Inn. The sight of the cutter dropping anchor and sending a boat ashore did not create as much of a panic as it had on the previous visit. Some were quick to spread the news, however. After a fine dinner, the three of them went back to the tavern to Cole and Anne's room.

Phillip smiled, "A far cry from Belcastle, but compared to the cutter, it's a palace."

Over the evening meal, Phillip had discussed the apprehension of a gang of smugglers at Hastings. Cole took a deep breath and then blurted out, "I'd not brag so about that." Phillip was taken aback at Cole's outburst.

Cole looked at his brother. "Did you get the man in charge, emphasizing the?"

"No," Phillip admitted.

"So, what you did was to send a bunch of men trying to make a little extra for their family to prison. You've seen the shops here in Deal. You've drunk ale and wine here at the tavern. Did you know the majority of it is smuggled?"

Phillip's mouth was wide open. "Cole, don't say that."

"I am going to say it and you're going to listen and keep your mouth shut about what I tell you. Did you know that the presents I bought mother and Catherine are smuggled goods? The tea, cigars, and the pipe tobacco our fathers smoke are smuggled. The fine wine is as well. Phillip, it's all smuggled. Did you know that an ordinary man can make ten shillings working a single night?"

Phillip knew that most people only made seven to ten shillings a week, if lucky.

Cole paused and then said, "There are some louts who drink and whore it away, but most of them use it for their families. Your brother routinely rotates smuggled goods in Uncle Angus's storeroom. It's the people who get hurt when you raid these landings, and they are not even the ones in charge. If they are caught they don't have the money to get out of trouble. Now I'll admit that not all the smugglers are people I'd care to socialize with. I recently shot one. But they're not all like the Hawkhurst gang either." Cole paused again for a moment. He wasn't too sure that he'd not gone too far. "I know you have to do your duty, Phillip. I wouldn't have you any other way. But remember, if our government didn't put such high taxes on things, there'd be no profit in smuggling and the average family could afford to buy things for the house and for their children."

Phillip had turned pale. Cole continued, "I didn't mean to shock you, brother. I just wanted you to know that there are two sides to everything."

"I'd never have believed it, Cole, had it not come from you. I have to think on this. My own brother involved with smugglers."

"No, Phillip, not involved with; just knowledgeable of the situation. I'd wager if he'd tell you the truth, that Captain Letchworth could tell you pretty much everything that I just did."

A knock was heard at the door. It was Chloe, and Phillip suddenly smiled. "An angel appears to calm the troubled sea."

Anne looked at Cole, a big smile on her face.

Cole said, "Was there something you needed, Chloe?"

She replied, never taking her eyes off of Phillip, "There's an officer here to return your horse, sir."

"Thank you, Chloe. We'll be right down."

"Here," Phillip said, speaking to Chloe as he offered his arm.

"A timely interruption," Anne whispered, "and then added an angel."

Cole shushed her as they followed his brother and Chloe out the door.

✵✵✵

A SLIGHT BREEZE BLEW AND the smell of fresh baked bread lingered in the air. This was an improvement over the smell of the fish market that had been notable that morning. It seemed much cooler. Apollo was running around the paddock kicking up his heels.

"He needs riding," Anne suggested.

Uncle Angus, Aunt Florence, and Sidney were due back from London today. Cole's stint as proprietor would be over. It had been a fast week. Most of the patrons had discussed the smugglers getting caught for all of a day, and then the talk of the war had returned. No other notes had been left, but Cole kept his pistols in his waistband.

During the time that Phillip's cutter was anchored in the Channel, he'd begged Cole to give Chloe a couple of days off. He bought her a dress from Dan Thompson and took her to the Blue Post Inn for dinner. There was a distinct change in Chloe after Phillip had gone back to duty.

At night, Cole saw her looking toward the entrance of the tavern at different times as if expecting Phillip to show up. "Phillip has brought a change in Chloe," Cole said to Anne.

"She's in love. I know how she feels. I felt the same way after meeting you only..."

When Anne didn't finish, Cole asked, "Only what?"

"She knows that with Phillip, being the son of a peer, she'll never be able to marry him. I knew from the beginning I'd have you, that we could be married."

"I never thought of that," Cole said.

"No and neither did Phillip," Anne said sharply. "Chloe is not your Meg offering favors for the fun of it. She is in love, madly in love. Yet knowing the most she could hope for with Phillip or someone like him is to be their mistress."

Damnation, Cole thought, Anne's comments are bitter but true. "I shall talk to Phillip about it when next we meet," Cole replied.

Anne nodded, but in her heart she wondered if it were not too late. Suddenly, she felt a chill; a tremble, an unexplained sensation. Was it in regards to Chloe, or was it about herself? Could she be pregnant, at the age of sixteen? She hoped not, not with Cole going to join his unit soon. But what if she was? She'd have his son...or daughter to hold while he was gone. She'd have her family close by. But what of Chloe; and then an idea came to her. Linda would take her in, but if not, she'd take Chloe in if she were pregnant.

***

RESTOCKING THE CIGAR BOXES FOR his uncle, Cole picked up a flyer that someone had left and read it. The Assize court convened February 1st in London at Old Baileys. A flyer was printed after the trials, called the proceedings. Cole remembered the headings on the first one he'd seen.

NEWS FROM NEWGATE

OR

AN EXACT AND TRUE ACCOUNT OF THE

MOST REMARKABLE

TRYALS

OF SEVERAL

NOTORIOUS MALEFACTORS

AT THE GOAL DELIVERY OF NEWGATE HOLDEN

FOR THE CITY OF LONDON AND COUNTY OF

MIDDLESEX.

The flyer went on to list the crimes of the villains, some of it very graphic and explicit, especially the sex crimes. A few of those being tried had lawyers, but most of them didn't. Cole's father had said if you find yourself to be tried at Newgate, you better hope you've a friend who can bribe your way out of trouble, or bribe a judge to sentence you to deportation. It's a short rope and a long fall, otherwise. Two of those tried were the Deal smugglers. If Stephenson was involved, Cole was sure that Martin would have a lawyer, or some guarantee that he'd not be prosecuted.

Joe had said sometimes a deal is made with a man that while he faced death, he'd die knowing that his family would be well taken care of.

"How good is that bargain?" Cole asked.

"I only personally know of one, but it's been held in its entirety," Joe replied.

Sir William's coach took him and Captain Letchworth to London for the trial. It went as expected for Martin. The other one sent for trial was killed for trying to coax a woman to have sex with him, not knowing that her husband was close by. The public laughed when the reason for his nonappearance was given, but Cole didn't think it was funny at all. He even wondered if it was the right body. One of the constables identified the rogue's body. Could this have been an example of the bribery that his father had talked about?

The crowd acted like it was a carnival or fair outside the courthouse. Cole was glad when Sir William, Captain Letchworth, and himself were ready to depart. It just didn't seem right that such solemn affairs were treated as a lark. He was thankful that Anne had not argued to come along.

CHAPTER THIRTY SEVEN

OLE HAD GOTTEN HIS LETTER instructing him to report on February 22nd. A messenger had delivered the letter along with a note from Major Huntington. Samuel had said if he'd like to come to Canterbury any day before the 20th, they could report together and he'd ensure that Cole met no undue obstacles.

Anne said that she wanted to go with Cole to Canterbury, so they planned to leave Deal on the 14th. Her parents would come over on the 19th.

Anne made love to Cole like she'd never done before that night. Not even on their wedding day had she been as aggressive and giving. Afterwards, Anne cuddled in Cole's arms.

He felt the wetness of her tears touch him. "We both knew the day was coming," he said, saddened to see his wife weep.

"Shut up," she hissed, as she kissed him fervently, snuggling even closer.

Cole felt like crying himself, knowing that he'd be leaving Anne behind soon. At some point sleep finally came.

Cole felt like he'd just closed his eyes when the smell of breakfast being cooked woke him. Anne lay beside him, her hair covering most of the pillow. Cole drew back the blankets and, seeing his wife's beautiful breasts, he leaned over, kissed first one nipple and then the other. He realized Anne was awake and watching him, as he rose up.

"How I wish I could wake up like this every morning for the rest of my life," she said.

"That would be wonderful," he said and smiled. "Now rise up, dear lady, and let's go break our fast."

Once in the dining room, Cole informed his aunt and uncle of their expected departure date.

"It will be a sad day in Deal, there's no doubt about it," Angus said. "I brought a boy with me to work and he leaves a man who has taught his uncle a lesson or two. I don't know of anyone who won't be missing you, lad."

Joe didn't come in that morning, so Cole made a decision to go visit him.

"I'm going," Anne said.

"You sure?" Cole asked.

"Yes, I'm going to spend every minute I can with you."

"We'll leave at midday then," Cole said. Sidney helped Cole with the saddling of Apollo and Anne's mare.

The road was unusually busy that morning with farm wagons, coaches, people on horseback, and people walking. Riding a bit further, it dawned on Cole that it was the start of Market Week.

"I am going to get a set of britches and ride like the girl we just passed," Anne said.

A boy and a girl, likely farmer's children, had ridden by, riding double on a horse, heading into Deal.

"She looked a lot more comfortable than I feel," Anne declared.

Cole, not knowing what to say, just nodded his head. Riding side-saddle was not something that he'd want to do, but it was considered the polite way for ladies to ride.

When they arrived at the Stuarts' farm, Joe was not there.

"He's at the warehouse," John had whispered. "Were you alone, I'd tell you to go there but not with your wife being with you. I'll go let him know that you're here."

Cole thanked John. Mary invited the two in for tea and she had baked both cookies and apple tarts.

"I'll take a tart," Cole said, not feeling bashful at all.

The sound of horses in the yard could be heard before long. Joe had been working to the point that he'd built up a sweat. It suddenly dawned on Cole. They are moving supplies out so there's likely to be a landing tonight or tomorrow. After an hour of friendly conversation, Cole and Anne mounted their horses. Just at the lane that went to Linda's and the warehouse, two heavily laden wagons pulled out. One of the drivers recognized Cole and waved. Paddy O'Hare and two men on horseback were bringing up the rear of the wagons.

Paddy pulled up but the other two men waved and followed the wagons. It didn't go unnoticed to Cole that they were armed with muskets and saddle pistols, but he didn't let on that he saw it.

"Out for an afternoon ride with your beautiful bride, are you," Paddy said, removing his hat and giving Anne a bow.

"I've gotten my orders to report," Cole said. "I just wanted to come by and let Joe know we'd be leaving soon."

Paddy gave a sigh. "You'll be missed, Cole. I don't know a soul who doesn't respect you. You've been a true friend, lad."

A black man turned in the lane, at that time, throwing his hand up. Cole waved back, "'Day to you, Saul."

"Linda has a good man in that one," Paddy said. Flushing, Paddy thought that he may have spoken out of place. "I'll be by to see you before you leave," he said and galloped off.

"Linda lives down that lane?" Anne asked.

"Yes," Cole replied.

Anne pulled her mare around and, without another word, she took off down the lane. Cole, too shocked to respond, sat on Apollo for a couple of moments before taking off down the lane after his wife. Cole sighted her pulling up into Linda's yard. Too late to head her off, dammit.

As Cole pulled in, he saw Saul struggling with a corner post at the wagon shed. He rushed over to give Saul a hand. With the two of them, it was easier to fit the new pole in place and dislodge and remove the old one.

Taking a piece of timber, Saul bumped the new pole into place. "Thank you, Cole; I can get it from here."

"My pleasure, Saul. I've seen this done at our stables a few times."

Cole had to catch his breath as he turned. Linda and Anne were talking and then Linda took Anne's hand and together they went into her house. They paused at the door.

"Cole, come in when you finish."

Damme, they act like sisters, Cole thought. Wishing that Saul needed him further, Cole could find no obvious reason to delay or put off his going in. Taking a deep breath, he gathered his courage and headed for the door. Entering the house, he found them at the kitchen table as Marge poured what looked like sherry into two small glasses.

"All I have to offer other than tea is wine, sherry, or brandy," Linda said.

Cole wasn't sure if Anne had ever had sherry before but after drinking their fill of tea at the Stuarts', he understood her wanting to try something different.

"Brandy will be good," Cole said, still somewhat anxious being in the company of his wife and ex-lover.

The two of them were chatting away, so Cole walked into the drawing room. Seeing an old copy of the London Gazette, he picked it up and started to read it. He was not surprised to see a list of hangings, which included Martin's. However, most of the paper, including the front page was dedicated to the war. One editor, in particular, wondered if Parliament was doing all it could to prevent the war. The article had gone on to say another war would bankrupt the nation.

"Cole...Cole." Looking up, both Linda and Anne were standing at the door.

"It's getting late," Anne said. "We need to go or it will be dark before we get to Deal." Cole got up and walked over to the door.

"You simply must come back," Linda said to Anne. "You don't know how refreshing it's been talking to you."

The two women kissed and then Linda turned to Cole and gave him a kiss on the cheek. "It's easy to see how you've fell so hopelessly in love with Anne. She is a darling."

Riding back to town they rode close enough together to hold hands.

"It's easy to see how you fell for Linda," Anne said. "She is absolutely stunning."

"You liked her," Cole said, never believing the two would ever speak, or let alone be friends.

Smiling Anne said, "Oh yes. I thanked her for sending me the letter. You know, Cole, I'm not surprised she...had a relationship with you. She's stuck out there alone, but for her servants. Not wanting to marry but needing a man; someone who could be discreet and not become possessive. Then you came along. You know, Cole, I could feel it in my heart, my very soul, as she talked about the needing part. I might be a wanton wench but there were times had we been alone, I'd have torn my clothes off to bed you."

"And I you," Cole replied.

Anne looked at her husband a minute. She was thinking but not saying, but you ran to Linda while I suffered. I am a bit jealous, Anne realized. But who wouldn't be. Linda would turn any man's head. But she thought to herself, I got Cole. He's my man now. But if he ever dallies again, I'll cut his nutmegs off. This caused to her to chuckle.

"What is so funny?" Cole asked.

Thinking quickly, Anne said, "Your face when you saw me talking to Linda."

Cole smiled, "It was a tense moment."

CHAPTER THIRTY EIGHT

COLE AND ANNE WERE HAVING dinner with her parents at the Blue Post Inn, two nights later. They had been at Anne's parents' earlier that day and so Cole rode Apollo back to Deal, tying the horse to a post beside the inn. Anne rode in the carriage with her parents. She'd brought a few bags of clothing to take to Belcastle in a few days.

Agnes, who rolled the cigars for the tavern, had volunteered to do some sewing for Anne. A few buttons and one dress that seemed to be a bit short. Either she'd gotten taller or the material had shrunk. Agnes would put a lace hem at the bottom so that a new hem wouldn't be noticeable.

Taking Joe's advice, Cole continued to wear his pistols in his sash since the note threatening his wife and Sir William had been received. Nothing had been said when Cole had decided to put it on. He needed to get used to them, as he would be wearing them constantly if he went to war.

The dinner had been excellent as always. Kimberly had joined them, so it was nearly ten when they walked out of the inn. Henry had already taken Anne's bags down to the tavern, so it would only be her parents going back home. Cole and Anne would walk from the inn to the tavern.

Cole had just helped Mary into the carriage as Sir William gave his daughter a hug. When he stepped up to be seated in the carriage, a shot rang out. Sir William's hat flew off and a ball thudded into the padded seat back.

Cole shoved Anne down while yelling for Mary and Sir William to get down. "Are you hit?" he asked. They both shook their heads no. "Stay behind the carriage and get back inside," Cole yelled.

Cole thought that he could see the remainder of a cloud of smoke, across the street. He ran to Apollo, and reached into the saddle bag, removing his other pistol. Swinging into the saddle he charged to where he'd seen the smoke. He rode down the alleyway, with his cocked pistol in his hand. He slowed down at an intersection, looking up and down the alley.

He heard the clatter of horse's hooves, so Cole dug his heels into Apollo and took off toward the sound. The sound was clear at first, and then it diminished. He's on the road, Cole decided. Putting Apollo into a gallop he reached the road. He didn't see a rider but there was dust headed toward the Dover Road. Digging his heels into Apollo's side, the horse took off. Cole saw the dust on the road grow thicker, making him believe that he was on the right track.

He now had Apollo in an all out run. It would have been thrilling were it not such a serious matter. The assassin was headed in the same direction as on the previous chase, Cole realized. He leaned forward until he was almost lying on Apollo's neck. His horse was fairly flying. Looking to the left, Cole saw the flash of a light. 'Shat' he thought, 'another landing.' The rogue had planned his escape during a time when any pursuit would encounter armed resistance. Could he catch the man in time? Whispering to his mount, he urged the stallion on.

They were closer now. The dust was much thicker, making it hard to see. Cole thought he could hear the sound of thundering hooves just ahead. How he wished for a blunderbuss or a shotgun; he could have chanced a shot. But with a pistol, it would only be a wasted shot. There he is, Cole thought. As they rounded a bend, Cole could see the man momentarily. They were getting closer but they were almost to the paths that led down the cliffs.

Apollo was lathered down and his breathing could be heard. I can't continue to push him, Cole knew. He'd not wind his beautiful stallion. If he didn't catch up within the next curve, he'd stop. He had decided to slow Apollo when he saw a line of wagons. Smugglers were lined up in the wagons ready for the tubmen to deliver their loads.

Cole saw a batman lift his musket as another looked toward a running man. Cole pulled back on the reins with one hand and waved the other hoping the batman would see he was not a duty man.

"It's me...it's me, Cole," he yelled as Apollo slid to a halt. Seeing Joe, he called, "Which way did that man go? He shot at us. nearly hitting Mary." Cole didn't want to mention Sir William.

"Down the path," Joe said.

Cole ran past him with Joe following. He soon met with tubmen coming up the path. He had to slow down for them. As he did so, he could hear an oomph, followed by shouts and curses. His prey had run into a tubman.

"Slow," Joe called behind him. "The path gets narrow and steep."

Yells could be heard just around the bend. The man was colliding with more tubmen. "Move aside," some of them yelled, followed by a line of curses.

Out at sea, in the channel, there was a bright orange flash, followed by the thunder of a cannon. It might have been a signal, but more likely it was a Customs boat firing on a smuggler craft. Shouts rang out for people to halt and hands up. This resulted in gunshots being fired and a general panic. Muzzle flashes were seen everywhere. Another person was knocked down amid the curses and gunshots.

"Get off me, ye clumsy bugger."

Cole saw the man rise up. He saw Cole at the same time. Both of the men shot, and behind Cole another shot was heard. Joe had shot as well.

"Lay down your arms in the King's name," a voice sang out. A voice that Cole recognized, it was Phillip's voice.

The call was answered by at least a dozen shots. Cole heard his brother cry out. He jumped over the man he'd been after.

There just off the path, he saw Phillip down on the ground. Lying around him were three other men. Sailors, from the look of their clothes. Cole pulled Phillip back from the path with Joe's help. It was hard to tell without a light, but it looked like a ball had grazed Phillip's head and one had gone through his arm. Joe tore the shirt from one of the dead sailors. Together he and Cole bound up Phillip's arm and head.

Once that was done, Joe looked at his young friend. "You are bleeding, Cole. Your shirt's bloody."

Cole looked down. His side hurt and now he felt faint. Joe pulled up his shirt. He wiped away most of the blood and leaned Cole forward.

"You've been shot. The ball went through you. That's good."

"Was it Eriksson?" Cole asked.

Joe shook his head, "No, it was Stephenson."

"Dalton's father?" Cole asked.

"Yes, he has purple scars down each side of his face. It was him that murdered Peg."

"But why shoot at you, Joe, and why the riding officer."

"He always wanted Linda, but she wasn't interested. He probably came after me knowing I vowed to kill the man who hurt Peg. Martin was Stephenson's half-brother. That's why he went after Sir William."

"Who do you think set the Customs men on his landing?"

"I think that was probably Eriksson. He lined up girls for Stephenson. When Peg was killed, Eriksson knew Stephenson would want him out of the way so he hid out in France."

"How do you know all this, Joe?" Cole asked.

"Paddy told me at the warehouse the other day. Eriksson sent the money to a man in Folkstone, who knows Paddy. It was Paddy who gave the money for drinks at the pub."

Cole replied, "He took a chance."

"Not much, those Irishmen stick together."

The shots and shouts had stopped and all seemed quiet.

"Let's get Phillip and head to the top," Cole said, grimacing as he stood.

"Let me bind you up first," Joe said.

As Joe was using a shirt from another dead sailor to bind up Cole's wound, Sergeant Duncannon came up the path with a squad of men.

"Who's there?" he bellowed.

"Cole, Sergeant."

Taking a torch from one of his men, he held it so that he could see. "So it's you again."

"I'm afraid so. Joe and I were chasing the assassin, only this time we got him. He's over there dead."

"And ya just happened to run him down in another of our operations."

"I didn't know you had an operation going on. But the rogue shot at Sir William at the Blue Post Inn. I chased him here." He added as an afterthought then, "I came up on Joe just outside of town and he helped give chase. But enough of that, though. My brother is here and he's been wounded a couple of times. Lend a hand so that we can get him to a doctor."

Sergeant Duncannon shined the torch on Phillip and then noticed Cole's side. "Looks like you've caught one yerself."

Cole nodded, "It was Stephenson. You'll find where Peg clawed him before he killed her. Joe and I both got a ball in him."

A torch was held over Stephenson for the men to see the claw marks on his face. One of the men spit on Stephenson's body.

"That's for Peg. She was a good girl."

Captain Letchworth was there by the time they got to the top of the road and, surprising Cole, so was Sir William. He had taken Anne's mare. Water was splashed over Phillip's face and he came to.

An Army surgeon was there and he looked at Phillip and Cole, stating that they needed care but would likely live. He said this with a smile, but Cole didn't see the humor in it.

When Sir William approached Cole, Cole said, "It was Mr. Stephenson. He still has the claw marks on his face Peg gave him." He quickly added, "I came up on Joe entering town. He helped me give chase."

Cole was glad when no one asked about the horses, but Joe smartly tied Apollo and Stephenson's horse to the back of the wagon they were taking back to town.

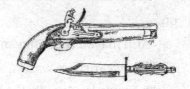

EPILOGUE

WHEN THEY GOT TO DOCTOR Garrett's office, they helped Phillip in. While waiting on the doctor to finish with Phillip, Anne rushed in, throwing her arms around Cole.

"I have been worried sick," she cried.

"I couldn't have somebody taking shots at my family."

Anne smiled, "No, you couldn't."

Phillip walked out at that time. "The doctor said had you not bound me up, brother, I'd likely bled to death."

Cole smiled, "Joe helped."

"I need to get word back to my ship," Phillip said.

"I'll take care of that," Sir William offered. "I'll take you to the tavern and get you in bed while Cole is being treated."

"I'll do that," Angus said. "I'll come back for Cole after getting Phillip to bed."

"I'll be heading home," Joe said. "Let me know if I'm needed."

Cole held out his hand, "Thank you, Joe." Shaking Cole's hand, Joe left.

"That's Stephenson's horse that Joe's on," Sir William said.

"Joe's must have run off," Cole said, "with all the shooting going on."

"And maybe there never was one," Sir William responded.

"I'll swear there was," Cole said.

"I doubt that it will ever be brought up," Anne's father said with a smile. "I'm glad that you got the assassin, Cole, but it was foolish taking out after him that way."

"I'd not have Anne put at risk again if I can help it; nor you or her mom."

"You are a brave man, Cole Buckley. Just remember you may not always be so lucky."

***

PHILLIP WAS TAKEN BACK TO the cutter the following afternoon. His arm was in a sling and he had a bandage on his head. Determined not to use a bosun's chair, he was more or less pushed into the cutter by some of the men.

Captain Atwater was like a mother hen taking care of his midshipman. "Captain Best will never forgive me if I bring Phillip back broke," he japed.

Cole was sore but thought he could tolerate the ride to Canterbury in the Brabham's carriage. He whispered to Anne, "If I was able to survive your ministrations last night and wake up wanting more, I think I can travel."

Anne smiled, "It's amazing what tricks you can find in a penny novel or learn from an older, experienced woman."

Cole rolled his eyes back, "You shock me, wench."

Anne leaned over and kissed him, whispering, "Wait until you get well."

Cole received a hero's welcome at Canterbury. Anne's father had written a letter and sent a courier so that Cole's family wouldn't be shocked. He also wrote a letter to Cole's commanding officer outlining Cole's actions and subsequent wounds. He also recommended one Joseph Lando as a likely sergeant for the newly formed regiment, citing his experience handling men and his courage under fire. He omitted that Joe was involved with the owlers at Deal.

It was not surprising to learn that the Earl had given his consent for Catherine and Major Samuel Huntington to be wed. In fact, the general in command of the new regiment had accepted an invitation to the wedding from the Earl. He had also extended the major and Cole's reporting date until March 20th.

One month later, on April 20, 1792, war with France was declared.

HISTORICAL NOTES

Kent: During the 18th century, when the economy of Kent and Sussex went into decline, the gap between the rich and the poor was vast. If a man was fortunate enough to work, he might make seven shillings a week. Trying to provide for a family with that amount of money was very difficult. However, that man could make ten shillings in one night by joining the smugglers.

Smuggling was made profitable due to the high taxes on several goods. Among these were tea, spirits (brandy in particular), tobacco and lace. It has been documented more contraband, such as tea, tobacco, and spirits were used by London society than those taxed.

The amounts of cash needed to fund a smuggling operation were huge. Kentish smuggling was on a scale that demanded large amounts of venture capital. The capital was often raised by investors. many of whom were in London.

The number of men needed to land a cargo of goods was enormous, often sixty to one hundred men.

Smuggling gangs were usually made into four groups of men, not including the main smuggler, whose identity was usually only known by a few trusted lieutenants. While some were known by the government, proof was hard to produce. The below is a breakdown of the smugglers' jobs:

The spotsman – this man would direct the cargo laden ships ashore using predetermined signaling.

A lander – this was the man that arranged the unloading of the cargo.

A tubsman – men who carried the goods, usually from a harness or tub strapped over the back and chest.

A bats man – these were the men that protected the tubsmen. They were usually armed with clubs and pistols.

Landfall: The master of a free trade ship was expected to not only land cargo but to do it at a preset timetable. While the timetable was fixed, the landing spot may vary due to the activities of the Customs men. This is where the spotsman earned his keep, directing a landing away from Customs men.

Borrowing horses: The need for horses to transport smuggled goods was huge. Therefore, horses were borrowed from farmers and landowners. A meaningful wink from a known smuggler friend indicated the stable doors should be left open. In the morning, the horse would be returned, often showing signs of overnight use but there'd be a keg of brandy or something the farmer liked left where it could be found.

The Riding Officer – The main duty of the riding officer was to patrol a section of the coast in order to suppress smuggling. He interacted with other riding officers he met during his rounds. He kept a journal reporting all activities to the Customs officers.

The Buffs or the Royal East Kent Regiment was an infantry regiment of the British Army garrisoned at Canterbury.

To purchase a commission in the cavalry or infantry required a sum of money be deposited with the relevant regimental agent. Commissions could also be bought from the government or from an officer desiring to sell his commission. In addition to the money to purchase a commission, letters of recommendation also had to be included. Just because a man had the money, the purchase of a commission may not be granted if the colonel didn't think the individual met a certain criteria that ensured the man met the social requirements needed to be an officer.

Market Week: When Market Week rolled around, buyers and sellers from nearby villages came to the town sponsoring the event. In the 1700's, there were only 800 market towns in all of England and Wales. People would come from all over the countryside. Farmers brought livestock as well as produce. Fishermen sold oysters, fish, and eels. Bakers sold bread and some merchants sold trinkets that they'd made. Booths were set up to sell beer and ale. There were gamblers and entertainment such as the boxing match in this book.

The Covent Garden: I have a book describing London as the most sinful city in the world in the 18th century. If that was true, the Covent Garden was the center of the sin. A book was actually written describing the specific specialties of each prostitute and the price for each activity. It was called Harris's list and reprinted copies are still available today. Several children were born to madams who were brought into the trade very early. A twelve year old girl's virginity usually brought a high price at auction. It was estimated that an overwhelming number of children were involved in London's sex market, at the time. The alternative was to starve.

About the Author

MICHAEL AYE IS A RETIRED Naval Medical Officer. He has long been a student of early American and British Naval history. Since reading his first Kent novel, Mike has spent many hours reading the great authors of sea and historical fiction, often while being "haze gray and underway" himself. His website is https://michaelaye.com/.

About the Illustrator

MIKE BENTON IS A LONGTIME friend of the author. His art can be found on his website: https://fineartamerica.com/profiles/mike-benton.